Juma the Great

# Juma the Great

By

## A.K. Chesterton

**The A.K. Chesterton Trust**

**2015**

Printed and published in 2015. Third Edition.

© **The A.K. Chesterton Trust**, BM Candour, London, WC1N 3XX, UK.

**Website**: www.candour.org.uk

**ISBN**: 978-0-9932885-3-1 (Paperback)
**ISBN**: 978-0-9932885-4-8 (Hardback)

Originally published in 1947.

Illustrations by Bernard W. Bays

# Dedication.

To Reginald Malkin, staunch campaigner, loyal comrade and one of the best and wittiest of men.

# I. SEDUCTION

On a day in the middle of 1940 War stretched forth a tentacle into the remote fastnesses of Uganda and brought Headman Juma, his two brothers and his five cousins into its toils.

Juma watched with impassive mien the arrival of the motor vehicle which had bumped over the plains and climbed the rough mountain tracks to reach his village. It was not the first he had seen, and even had it been he would not have allowed himself to be unduly impressed. Such magical contrivances did not infringe upon his world, bringing neither increase nor decrease of wives, or cattle, or crops, and were therefore to be regarded with the detachment becoming to a Baganda nobleman.

Out of the vehicle jumped a spruce British recruiting officer.

"Greetings O Juma!"

"Greetings, Bwana."

The headman led his visitor to a reception hut, where they sat and talked of many things. Juma's eyes were fixed upon the officer's broad slouch hat, turned up, colonial fashion, at one side. What would he not give to possess so superb a canopy! Then there came the proposition – the startling, lunatic proposition.

"Juma", said the officer. "The Government is going to send an army to fight the Italiani in the country of the Habashi, and your help is needed. I have been sent to ask if you will become an askari and drive a lorry for the Government."

Juma looked with startled eyes at his visitor, convinced that he could not be quite right in the head.

"What strange talk is this, Bwana? I could not drive your carriages because I know nothing of such things."

"Oh, the Government will teach you how to drive", replied the tempter.

Juma shook his head. "The lorry would run away and I should not know how to stop it."

"The Government will teach you how to stop it before it teaches you how to make it go", said the recruiting officer, rallying his resources.

The Headman looked pityingly upon his interviewer, as upon a child. "How can that be, Bwana? It does not sound to me a possible thing to make a lorry stop before it has been made to go."

"You'll very soon pick up the idea. Why, there are a lot of Baganda now in Nairobi learning to drive."

That did not interest Juma. The folly of other men was not his concern.

"Think what it would mean", continued the officer. "You will be driving into the Abyssinian country as an askari, and the women of the Habashi are very beautiful."

The Headman pondered this remark in silence. Yes, it was certainly true that the Habashi women were famous for their beauty.

"Then there is the question of pay. The pay is good and will enable you to save much money and buy fine new wives when you come back. If you become a sergeant you would receive one hundred shillingi a month."

Juma had some idea of the value of money. "I would be paid one hundred shillingi a month?" he asked incredulously.

There was a struggle in the officer's soul between his zeal and his honesty. The latter won.

"Well, if you become a sergeant you would", he replied. "In addition the Government will give you your food and your uniform, and you would have the high status of an askari, and the Government would be very pleased with you."

Juma's mind was concentrated on the word "uniform". He looked again at his visitor's head and leant forward with sudden eagerness. "Bwana", he asked breathlessly, "Would I wear a big askari hat like yours?"

"Of course. It is part of the uniform."

In a state of some excitement Juma rose, saying that he must talk the matter over with his wives. But the real reason for seeking his own hut was a temptation to take a whiff of bhang. Such a whiff, he always maintained, cleared his head and enabled him to arrive at wise decisions, which was a fallacy. For bhang, being an intoxicating drug, had the invariable effect of making him quite beatifically tight.

As the fumes stole into his brain Juma reviewed the amazing proposition put in front of him – the proposition to become a god in control of one of these miraculous chariots, to receive one hundred shillingi a month (his mind nimbly leapt over the qualifying clause), to drive as a conqueror into the Abyssinian country, to gather unto himself the grateful, admiring smiles of the Habashi women, and above all to move about the world surmounted by a huge, heroic askari hat. Life could hold no more magnificent destiny for any man.

He hurried back lest the officer should change his mind. "Bwana", he said and his tongue lovingly caressed each enchanted word. "Bwana, I will come with you and drive a gari and I shall bring with me my two brothers and five cousins, and they shall all drive garis, and we will go and fight the Italiani in the land of the Habashi, and the Habashi women will smile at us, and when we come back we shall buy many wives, and the Government will be very pleased with us."

Next day, Juma, his two brothers and five cousins, were being bumped in a lorry across the great plains on their long safari to Nairobi. Juma's indulgence in bhang had led to a hang-over. As he watched the mountains of his native land recede from view, he scratched his head and morosely examined his heart.

"What the hell", he asked himself in his own idiom, "what the hell have I gone and let myself in for now."

## II. REACTION

Recruit-Driver Juma's depression accompanied him to Nairobi and abode with him some days after his arrival at the cantonments. Next morning, indeed, it reached depths rarely experienced in his tranquil life in the hills.

He and his kinsmen, and a horde of Wakamba recruits – Juma spat at the sight of them – were awakened at five o'clock, and instead of being taken straight to the vehicle-lines to learn how to drive lorries, they were formed up on the parade ground and made to do the most senseless, maniacal things.

Juma found himself obliged to leap up and down, to swing his arms in every direction, to stretch his neck, to bend his body, to lie down on his stomach and to raise himself up and down on his hands, to lie on his back and wave his legs ludicrously in the air – there was no end to these fantastic contortions, all of which sadly wounded the dignity becoming to a Baganda nobleman. In the company of the despised Wakamba, too!

During the break he walked apart with his brother Matua.

"Is this how we drive lorries for the Government?" wailed Matua.

"There is one good thing", came an answering growl from Juma. "Our wives are far away and cannot see what fools the Government make of us."

"Truly", said Matua.

Then the whistle blew for further irrelevant imbecilities. The squad was divided into two parties facing each other, both in two ranks. The rear rank men were instructed to mount on the backs of the front rank and the two parties then charged into the fray, it being the business of the horsemen to unseat his opposite number by pulling him to the ground.

Juma, with lowering face, was carried forward as a horseman into the battle, but he had decided on passive resistance. He refused to soil his hands by clutching at the body of a despised M'kamba[1], and not for the world would he humiliate a fellow-Muganda by laying him in the dust. No, not for a hundred shillingi a month, and at present he was only to draw fifteen shillingi.

While thus poised aloft and passive everywhere save in his heart, Juma was taken in his rear; strong arms caught him by the head, and in a split second he was sprawling on the parade ground. He sprang up to confront his grinning victor.

"You dog of a Kamba!" he roared. "You misbegotten son of a hyaena—"

But before he could launch his private war, the whistle blew, the ranks were reformed and it was now Juma's turn to be a horse. No longer passive, but raging belligerent, he charged blindly forward, came into collision with another couple and all four were sent sprawling, Juma on his lip.

He got up with mutiny in his heart. It was not the bleeding mouth that worried him, but the culminating blow to his *amour propre.*

"Is it thus that one drives a lorry for the Government?" he shouted at the top of his voice, in a tone of stupendous indignation. The only reply was a shout of laughter from the hated Wakamba, to whom all these things which so distressed the Baganda had been fun and games of the very first water. Thereafter there was no refuge for poor Juma, except in thoughts of murder – grand, satisfying, wholesale murder.

---

[1] In these tribal names the reader should remember that Swahili words change their case at the beginning. He will not be confused if he refers to the stem, which for the sake of simplicity I sometimes use without prefix. – Author.

If the rest of the day spared Juma further physical indignities, it did nothing to diminish his sense of the Government's fatuous absurdity.

Thus for a whole hour he was made to carry his left foot away from his right and then bring it back again.

"Squadi – shun! standa – ease! Squadi – shun! standa – ease!" yelled the big Kamba drill-instructor with maddening iteration. "Squadi – shun! standa – ease!"

"I shall kill that man", reflected Juma. "And I shall kill the other man who made me jump up and down like a lunatic. And I shall kill the Bwana Recruiting Officer. And I shall kill all these unspeakable Wakamba . . ."

"Squadi – shun! standa – ease! Squadi – shun! standa – ease!"

"Has the great Wakamba ape no other song?" growled Juma to his brother Matua. "Why should a man not stand as please him best? Is it thus that that one learns to drive a lorry for the Government?"

It transpired, though not to Juma's peace of mind, that the drill-instructor did know other songs.

"Lef-turn! Right-turn! Lef-turn! Right-turn!"

"By God", he muttered to Matua, "Does this Wakamba wart-hog think that we do not know how to go to the left when we want to go to the left?"

"Lef-turn!" roared the instructor, and Juma executed a weary turn to the right.

# III. INITIATION

The Government neither repented nor relented. A week went by, and each day Juma found himself still jumping up and down, twisting and bending his body, left-turning, right-turning, until his thoughts of sudden murder gave way to day-dreams wherein he devised lingering deaths for his persecutors.

"Squadi - abou – turn! Abou-turn! Abou-turn! Abou-turn!"

"Does this baboon of a Wakamba think we do not know how to face the way we want to face?" he fumed to Matua.

Even the first driving lesson did nothing to appease his wrath or weaken his conviction that the Government was out of its mind.

The squad was marched up to a skeleton lorry placed upon some scaffolding, in order that they might learn the working of the various controls.

"Get up" said the Jaluo instructor to Juma, indicating the cab.

Juma looked at the dummy and then at the instructor, and it seemed that even Juma's very expressive eyes could not contain the full measure of his scorn.

"This is childishness", he announced.

"Shauri gani?" asked the instructor. "What's the matter?"

"I cannot drive this vehicle. Can you not see that it has no wheels? How can you make a lorry go when it has no wheels?"

"Get up!" snapped the Jaluo.

Juma gritted his teeth and obeyed. The instructor jumped up into the seat beside him.

"Now first of all", he explained, "I will show you how stop the vehicle quickly."

Juma remembered his argument with the recruiting officer and felt his logic on that occasion to be irresistible on this.

"How is one to stop a vehicle which one cannot even make to move?" he asked contemptuously.

The Jaluo instructor addressed him without anger. "You are a fool", he said, "and it is clear to me that both your mother and father were fools, and also your grandmothers and grandfathers. For only a fool and a son of fools would think to teach his instructor what he himself does not know. Now press your right foot down on that pedal – no, fool, your right foot."

Juma crashed a savage foot down on the pedestal and secretly added another name to his black list.

"That is the way to stop the vehicle quickly" said the instructor serenely. "If you always do that when in trouble you will save the Government much money."

Juma made a mental vow to indicate his opinion of the Government by never, never pressing that pedal either with his left foot or with his right.

"Now to start the machine", continued the instructor and he launched upon an exposition of the appropriate details.

Juma shrugged his shoulders. If this Jaluo maniac could not see that a machine without wheels could never be made to start he must be left to his delusions.

Even so he went mechanically thorough the idiotic movements required of him. He learnt to press the self-starter, to declutch, to go into first gear, to double declutch, to go into second gear, and so on up to fourth gear, and then to come back through each successive stage to neutral. After an hour his response to the instructor's orders had become automatic and perfect.

"Bas!" said the instructor. "Enough!"

They climbed out of the cab and on level ground again he looked at his pupil with satisfaction.

"Good!" he explained. "You have learnt quickly." Juma refused to accept this praise.

"I told you at the beginning", he said with an air of melancholy satisfaction.

"What did you tell me at the beginning?"

"I told you it was not possible to make a lorry move without wheels. Look! It is in the same place as when we started."

The instructor gave him a glance of mild curiosity. Then he summoned Matua into the cab.

Juma stared. "Does this rat of a Jaluo think Matua can do what even I cannot do?" he asked himself, and spat vehemently upon the ground.

# IV. EXULTATION

To the winter of every man's discontent there comes sooner, or later, the glorious summer of his balance and redress. Juma's came – the first flush of it – on the day when the uniforms were issued, for up to now the recruits had been obliged to wear the garments in which they had arrived.

They queued before the Bwana Quartermaster sergeant's store, Juma and his Baganda coterie in the rear. The Wakamba went in and emerged with khaki blouses, slacks, shorts, belts, vests, socks, boots, and – to Juma's infinite dismay – tarbushes. Was this the way the recruiting officer fulfilled his promise of a large askari sombrero! But the Baganda were lucky. Just as their turn arrived, the stock of tarbushes gave out, so that they all received the coveted slouch hats such as were worn by the proud K.A.R.

They raced back to their hut and changed with incredible rapidity. That the uniforms fitted where they touched did not matter to a soul. They clamped on their belts and adjusted the hats which were their crowning glory, surveyed each other and then themselves in a bit of broken mirror produced by Matua and were so satisfied with the result that they laughed with glee, shook hands and pranced up and down the hut with immense gusto in every stride. Now it was clear to all the world that they belonged to the order of the majestic and the brave.

They went out into the lines and swaggered past the despised Wakamba wearing the inferior tarbush and when there were no more Wakamba to swagger past a council of war was held as to what to do next. Clearly on such a superb occasion no parades could be expected of them.

*" they surveyed each other and then themselves "*

"Come", said Juma, "let us go into the village and show our uniforms to the women of Kikuyu."

This suggestion was loudly acclaimed and Juma lead the way to the village through a gap in the thornbush boma which enclosed the camp.

Half an hour later they arrived, like conquerors entering a beleaguered city. The effect was all they could have desired. Not a lady of the Kikuyu but glanced with admiration at these tall, handsome Baganda braves in their fine uniforms and rip-roaring hats. There were many smiles of welcome.

The occasion clearly called for drinks all round and it was not long before they found a place where Nubian gin was sold. Only the previous evening each recruit had received an advance of five shillingi, and thus there was enough money to finance a rollicking party.

Morning turned to afternoon, and in the afternoon Kikuyu ladies came crowding into the hut to feast their eyes upon the Baganda, who bought them drinks and still more drinks for themselves until all was high festival.

Juma found his soul swept by a wave after wave of the sheerest ecstasy. All the discords of the week vanished. The jumpings and body twistings and left and right-turnings that had so enraged him now took on bright hues and blended into the harmonious pattern of a bold askari life. In his present exultation and strength he believed he could even drive the wheel-less lorry in triumph as far as the gates of the sunset.

Not until six in the evening did anybody propose a move back to the camp.

"Good!" said Juma, leaping to his feet. "But we shall not go in the manner that we came. We shall march back."

That was a grand idea. Juma's two brothers and five cousins with half a dozen Baganda associates fell in outside and stood swaying in front of their leader, who swayed even more precariously than they. Their lady friends gathered round to watch the epic scene.

"Squadi – shun!" roared Juma, conscious of living in one of the great moments of his life. "Squadi lef-turn!"

As his followers all knew that the camp lay to the right they all turned to the right, precisely as Juma had intended. He was delighted.

"Squadi quick – march!"

It was a superb progress back to camp, containing more dynamic than one would have thought any march could hold.

No creeping through a hole in the boma this time. Straight up the road did Juma lead his prancing men and towards the main entrance where stood the Wakamba sentry.

So all-embracing was Juma's love of his fellow-men at that hour that he grinned amiably at the sentry and even greeted him – dog of a Wakamba that he was – as "brother".

The sentry responded by springing forward and pointing his bayonet at Juma's stomach, at the same time shouting for his companions. Out tumbled the guard, all with menacing bayonets, and before the men of that memorable march knew what had happened they were rounded up and flung into the guard-room.

They promptly fell asleep and thus were spared the anxiety of brooding upon what this abrupt ending to their day's festivities might portend.

"Squadi standa - ease", murmured Juma, turning over in his sleep and with the smile of the blessed on his lips.

# V. ADMONITION

Came the dawn, and with it a dozen Baganda headaches. Juma awaking looked around upon his unfamiliar surroundings.

"What's the matter?" he asked the Wakamba corporal of the guard. "What are we doing in this place?"

"It is a very bad affair", replied the corporal. "You are in big trouble and must go before the Bwana Mkubwa."

Recollection of the way his great gala day had been brought to an end stirred in Juma's mind and springing to his feet he brandished a fist in the corporal's face.

"Big trouble!" he shouted. "The only trouble is the mischief made by you half-witted Wakamba wart-hogs in bringing us here."

"Sit down and hold your noise", said the N.C.O. calmly. "Or else" – he indicated the butt of his rifle – "or else I will crack you over the head with this."

The corporal looked as though he meant it, and since his head was already intolerably sore Juma sat down and lapsed into a sultry silence.

Four hours later he and his dejected companions were thrust between an escort and paraded before the orderly-room. Here their magnificent hats were snatched off their heads. Deeming this a calculated robbery, Juma was about to enter a passionate protest when he caught a glimpse of the fierce moustache of the European sergeant-major.

His protest died gulping in his throat.

Prisoners and escort were then marched into the dread presence of the Bwana Mkubwa.

The major read out the names and numbers, starting with Juma.

"No. 389775 Recruit-driver Juma. Is that you?"

"Yes, Effendi", agreed Juma, witholding the mental reservation that the Bwana Mkubwa must be a feeble-minded person to ask such as question. "Who does he think I am if he does not think that I am myself?"

The charge was read out. It alleged that they had been absent without leave from 10.30 hours to 18.30 hours on the 17th August, 1940.

"Sergeant Wambua."

The hated Kamba drill-sergeant gave his evidence, asserting that these men had been absent from the 11 o'clock parade, the 2 o'clock parade and the 4.30 parade.

"Any questions to ask this witness?"

The only question that occurred to Juma was to ask Sergeant Wambua whether his mother had been a baboon or an orang-outang, but he felt that it might be prudent to leave it unasked.

"Corporal Onyango."

The detested Kamba corporal of the guard spoke up, describing how the festive party had been arrested on their return to camp.

"Any questions? No? Very well, what have you to say for yourselves?"

There followed an uneasy silence. Looking up, Juma found that the Bwana Mkubwa's full gaze directed upon him. Clearly the Bwana considered it was up to him to restore the situation.

"Effendi", he said. "It is not we who have made this affair. This affair has been made by the mischief of the Wakamba."

"Indeed? Do you mean that the Wakamba were absent without leave, and not you?"

"It is true we were in the village and not the Wakamba, Effendi", said Juma. "But if the Wakamba sergeant had not made a big noise, and if the Wakamba guard had not seized us when we came back, then all would have been well. There would have been no affair. Effendi, truly it is the Wakamba who have made this mischief."

The Bwana Mkubwa kept his steady gaze on Juma.

"Juma", he said. "I do not think you are a fool, although you talk exactly like one. In acting as they did the Wakamba sergeant and the guard were simply doing their duty. It is nonsense to say they have made this trouble. Absence without leave is a most serious crime. You are all of you new to the army and have still to learn its laws, so I will take a lenient view of your offence this time. But if you come before me again you will be severely punished. Admonished!"

"Escort and prisoners shun! Right-turn", bawled the sergeant-major. "Quick march."

Outside, Juma's equanimity was restored with the restoration of his beloved hat.

He sauntered away arm-in-arm with Matua.

"Your speech to the Bwana Mkubwa was excellent", said Matua.

"Yes", agreed Juma. "It was a good speech. Fortunately the Bwana Mkubwa is a very wise man. He did not punish us because he knows as well as we that it was the Wakamba who made all the mischief."

# VI. GRADUATION

Although Juma often talked like one, it was true, as Bwana Mkubwa had surmised, that he was not a fool. The trouble with him was that he was a man of stubborn preconceptions and the slave of overpowering moods. But when freed from these fetters his brain worked quite exceptionally well.

This was proven on the solemn and awe-inspiring morning when his squad was taken down to the great circuit on the plains and placed in the driver's seats of lorries which really did go. Hitherto, when pressing levers and buttons in the dummy cab, Juma had been convinced that the Government had no other purpose than to make an ass of him. Finding himself now confronted with the familiar controls, it suddenly dawned on him that he had learnt, in spite of himself, how to drive a vehicle.

In obedience to the Jaluo instructor beside him he pressed down the self-starter, declutched, went into first gear, accelerated, slowly released the clutch, and then to his wild delight the lorry moved off. He laughed with sheer joy.

Round and round the circuit he went, in company with about twenty other lorries, until the chief instructor blew two blasts of his whistle.

"Second gear", said the Jaluo, and Juma went through the necessary motions in compliance. He laughed again to find his lorry, like all the others, now going appreciably faster.

"Will it go faster in third gear?" he asked his instructor.

"Of course."

"Then I shall try third gear."

"No!" exclaimed the instructor sharply, knocking his pupil's hand off the gear-lever. "Fool! What kind of mess would you make in third gear when all the other garis are in second gear!"

Juma's face darkened. "Have I shown myself to be the man to make a mess?" he asked himself indignantly. "Have I not displayed that I am a superb driver? This dog of a Jaluo is jealous."

But he said nothing.

The whistle blew again.

"Now", exclaimed Juma triumphantly, "now the Bwana himself blows that we shall travel in third gear."

"No" rasped out the instructor. "First gear."

Juma obeyed, but not without muttering: "This is childishness. We have already been in first gear. What is the point of returning to it?"

Yet for an hour and upwards this is precisely what Juma and his fellow recruits did. They changed from first gear to second and back again throughout the period. Then came a break.

The recruits dismounted and ran to each other in ecstasy. Wakamba shook hands with Wakamba and Baganda with Baganda, all laughing and chattering and exultant with their own prowess. Only Juma walked gloweringly apart with Matua.

"The Government is without wisdom", he growled. "It does not know that in third gear these wonderful garis can travel very much faster than in second gear."

"Truly", replied Matua, to whom Juma's sayings were as Holy Writ.

During the rest of the morning, however, and throughout the whole of the afternoon and next day, the Government utterly declined to show a progressive spirit. First gear, second gear, first gear, second gear. Juma chafed and inwardly raged.

Not until the third day did the Bwana officer blow three blasts on his whistle and the Jaluo corporal utter the magic formula "third gear". Juma's left hand and foot responded with astonishing rapidity, and as the vehicle leapt forward he sat back in his seat and found it difficult to refrain from shouting his ecstasy to the skies. This was speed! This was power! This was life!

After several laps his ambition soared.

"Does the lorry go faster in fourth gear?"

"You will not drive in fourth gear until you are told", replied the instructor firmly.

Juma scowled. The wart-hog of the Jaluo existed only to cramp his style.

Back to second gear, down to first gear, up again to second. "We have done all these things", muttered Juma. "It is foolery to do them over and over again."

That afternoon, however, four blasts were sounded, and the order "fourth gear" was given, and almost at once things began to happen. Out of the corner of his eye Juma saw on the other side of the circuit a lorry crash into the rear of another. The vehicle in front then performed the same service for its immediate predecessor. There were two most satisfying crashes.

Juma's whole frame became animated and his heart sang. He had not realised that this glorious game of bumps-a-daisy formed part of the contract. But since it did, why he, Headman Juma, could engineer a first class smash as well as any man alive. He banged down on the accelerator and in his eyes was a visionary gleam as the machine leapt forward.

"Stop, you fool!" yelled the instructor.

Juma did not hear and did not intend to hear.

"Madman!" The instructor grabbed the handbrake and brought the vehicle to a halt within two feet of a collision.

"Madman!" The instructor glared at his pupil and treated him to the only two words of English he knew: "Bleedy Fool!"

Juma, cheated of his triumph, was about to grip the Jaluo saboteur by the neck when his attention was caught by the advent of the Bwana officer to address the Wakamba driver in front, who had achieved such a creditable crash.

The officer spoke long and fluently, and Juma could hear every word. As he listened, all other feelings melted into a mounting admiration for this officer. By the time the speech was over admiration had given way to hero-worship.

"These white men are indeed wonderful people", he remarked later to Matua. "They can swear at us in our own language better than we can swear ourselves."

"Truly!" said the faithful Matua.

"As for those two fools of Wakamba who smashed up their garis, they are not fit to be in charge of vehicles."

"Truly."

"For myself", concluded Juma. "I shall never smash up a lorry."

And for many thousands of miles of (nearly) impeccable safari Juma was as good as his word.

# VII. PROMOTION

Recruit-Driver Juma was in love. It was a polygamous love, for he took unto his heart every motor-vehicle that ever travelled on wheels. To drive one of them was the supremacy of bliss. But he was not content with driving. He made friends with the Jaluo corporal and spent hours with him bending over the entrails of these adorable machines. He learnt how they worked, how to doctor them when they were sick, how to maintain them and keep them clean.

He passed out of the recruits' course a second-class driver, being the only one to make this steep grade. He looked out upon the world with kind eyes.

The squad were packed into a couple of lorries and taken thirty miles from Nairobi to join the motor transport company to which they had been assigned. Here they were given practical work to do, carrying ammunition, petrol and supplies in convoy to Garissa – an all-round journey of five hundred miles in boiling heat.

No matter how harsh the sun, how bumpy the road, Juma behind his steering wheel was the happiest of men. He asked nothing better of life than to spend all his days driving, driving, driving, and in between times to doctor sick machines and put his rapidly acquired knowledge at the disposal of all other drivers, including even the hounds of the Wakamba.

But he was offered something better. There came a day when his Bwana officer sent for him.

"Juma", said the officer. "I understand you are a headman among your own people."

"Truly, Effendi," said Juma, gratified that his fame should have reached such august ears.

"You are very good driver", went on the other.

"Truly, Effendi."

"And you have learnt much about the maintenance of vehicles."

"Truly, Effendi."

"I think you are also a man of very strong character."

"Truly, Effendi." Juma's heart went out to this white man. Why, their ideas on all matters exactly coincided. They both spoke the same language. They were brothers.

"Therefore I have decided to jump you up straight away to the rank of full corporal. Go to the Bwana quartermaster-sergeant and he will let you have the stripes."

Juma had not been expecting anything of this kind. His emotion was almost too strong to be contained. Here he was, at one fell swoop, exalted to a position among the celestial beings. His face seemed to enlarge itself in order to capture the whole vast dazzle of his smile.

"Assahanti, Effendi", he said. "Thank you! Thank you very much indeed!"

He threw the whole of his rich emotional nature into a luscious salute. He saluted a second and third time, then turned and strode towards the quartermaster's hut, and as soon as he was out of sight he ran.

Half an hour later he arrived at the vehicle lines, with a feeling as of blood pounding through his biceps just underneath the brave new badges. He was unbelievably arm-conscious.

His Baganda comrades, delighted with the sight rushed forward to shake him by the hands. Even the Wakamba, forgetting his contempt and remembering only his assistance when they were in difficulty with their vehicles, grinned amiably at him.

Juma trod on air.

This was not a day such as other days. Nobody would expect him to devote himself to the humdrum task of maintenancing his vehicle on what was so clearly a gala occasion. What was more, nobody would contest his right, as a now acknowledged leader and great man, to excuse whomever he pleased from maintenancing their vehicles, so that he might go with him into Thika village, where he would display his dazzling stripes to the Thika ladies and buy his admirers large quantities of Nubian gin.

Juma and his Baganda followers were soon trailing along the path through the bush, adding yet another to the countless billions of examples which show how men insist, in joy and in sorrow, upon repeating the pattern of their lives.

It was not until afternoon that Sergeant Kangata – fate decreed that he, too, should be of the Wakamba – came round the vehicle lines and discovered that none of the Baganda vehicles were being maintenanced.

"Where is Corporal Juma?" he enquired.

"He has gone to the village", replied the Wakamba drivers, who were deeply hurt at being left behind.

Sergeant Kangata went and reported to Bwana[2] Sergeant Robinson, and Bwana Sergeant Robinson went and reported to the Bwana officer.

---

[2] Bwana – Lord. Indicates a European.

"Tell Sergeant Kangata to take a couple of lorries and a search party of twenty men down to Thika and round the blighters up", said the officer.

The search party duly set forth, and eventually came upon Juma and his festive companions in a Nubian gin shop, just as had been expected.

When the Wakamba put in an appearance the Baganda leapt unsteadily to their feet with eyeballs rolling – a sure sign that they were not very far removed from frenzy.

"What do you Wakamba jackals want in this place?" demanded Juma, a drunken menace in his voice.

Sergeant Kangata saw that this was a situation demanding tact.

"We have brought two lorries for you, Corporal Juma", he said. "The Bwana officer sent us".

Corporal Juma's truculence immediately dissolved into a smile of enormous complacency.

"Observe", he said, addressing his followers. "Observe what privileges my promotion has brought you! Now that I am a great man the Bwana officer sends a lorry so that we may travel back to the camp in comfort. Come, let us return and thank him for sparing our legs."

The lorries arrived back at the vehicle lines resounding with the triumphant battle songs of the Baganda, those most privileged of men.

## VIII. DISSIMULATION

Came another dawn and another batch of Baganda headaches.

Two hours later Corporal Juma was standing before his Bwana officer.

"Juma", said the officer. "I am disappointed in you."

Juma hung his head.

"What excuse have you to offer?"

There was silence. Then the culprit remembered the excuse which had stood him in such good stead with the Bwana Mkumba in Nairobi.

"Effendi", he said. "This is a trouble made by the Wakamba."

"What have the Wakamba to do with it?"

"If Sergeant Kangata had not made such big noise you would have heard nothing about it."

"Well?"

"If you had heard nothing about it, Effendi, then there would have been no affair."

"This is foolish talk, Juma", said the officer. "Neglect of duty is always a big affair, even when it is not discovered. What would happen if you and your Baganda went off to Thika whenever you wanted and left your lorries to take care of themselves? It would mean

" What excuse have you to offer?"

that when we came to drive out against the enemy the lorries would break down, and you would be left behind in the bush while the army moved on. If the Italiani or the Somali Banda did not find you and kill you, the lions would."

"I know how to hunt lions, Effendi."

The officer was casting about in his mind for a suitable reply to this unexpected remark when the crash of a collision sounded in the adjacent bush.

Juma's reaction to such sounds never varied. He spat upon the ground and growled "Clumsy Wakamba fool", for in his philosophy nobody save the Wakamba ever crashed a lorry.

This time he spat with particular emphasis, for he welcomed the diversion.

The two of them walked rapidly to the scene of the accident.

There they found Matua in violent altercation with Amisi, a Kamba driver. Juma's indignation on behalf of his brother became immediately apparent.

"Look, Effendi!" he cried. "Look how this blind fool of a Kamba has crashed into Matua's lorry.

The officer went closer to inspect. "On the contrary", he said, "it seems to be Matua who has crashed into Amisi.

"That is what I say, Effendi," replied Juma, shifting his ground without a seconds hesitation. "If Amisi had not put his lorry in this place, then it would not have been in Matua's way and there would have been no affair."

The officer shot him a glance which he did not know how to interpret, so he busied himself helping to investigate the wreckage. Necessary action having been taken, he began to slide away into the bush.

"Stop!" Keen eyes had spotted him.

"Yes, Effendi."

"There remains the affair of yesterday. If it happens again you will no longer be a corporal".

"Yes, Effendi."

"Moreover, until you win back my confidence you will report to Sergeant Kangata every hour between sunrise and sunset. On no day will you fail to do this."

"Yes, Effendi."

"Send Sergeant Kangata to me so that I may tell him what I have just told you."

"Yes, Effendi."

Back in his own lines Juma was surrounded by Baganda compatriots. "How does the affair of yesterday stand?" they asked. "What are the punishments?"

"There are to be no punishments", he said loftily. "The Bwana officer is very angry with Sergeant Kangata for making his big noise about us. The Bwana said that the Wakamba sergeant has to be watched less he do other mischief, and it is my duty to go and watch him every hour between sunrise and sunset."

"Ow!" exclaimed the Baganda, terrifically impressed.

# IX. EVASION

Every hour between dawn and sunset for several days Juma kept faithful watch over the potential mischief of Sergeant Kangata, until a series of continuous convoys up the line relieved him of the task.

At first the Bwana officer would halt his convoy for the night at Mwingi in the Kitui Hills, the only inhabited place in a vast emptiness of bush. Then he noticed at Mwingi that when the N.C.O.'s reported for the next day orders before going to sleep, Juma always received his with singularly little attention, but with a wealth of gratitude.

"Thank you, Effendi. Thank you. Thank you very much indeed", Juma would say, with the beaming smile of a man admitted into paradise.

"You will see that each driver keeps half a gallon of reserve water supply for his radiator."

"Oh, thank you very much indeed, Effendi", from Juma.

"And check up on each driver's petrol."

"Oh, thank you very much indeed, Effendi"

"See that one hundred yards' distance between lorries is maintained."

"Good, Effendi. Thank you. Thank you very much."

On the third such Mwingi occasion the officer added: "And for you, Corporal Juma, I have a special instruction."

"Thank you, Effendi."

"To-morrow morning at dawn you have my permission to take a tow-rope and hang yourself from that tree."

"Oh, thank you! Thank you Effendi. Thank you very much indeed."

Thereafter, his suspicions confirmed, the officer would stop his convoy fifteen miles beyond Mwingi, a circumstance that robbed the Nubian gin-merchants of Juma's most esteemed custom, and Juma himself of his famous dawn headaches.

The result was that Juma prospered mightily in the land. He drove his vehicle with skill, he carefully maintenanced it, he ensured that all subordinates maintenanced theirs, and in this way not only won back his officer's confidence, but became known throughout the company as a keen, hard-working and reliable N.C.O.

Only once during this period was he tempted to leave the straight and narrow path, and out of this occasion he managed with consummate cleverness and luck to fashion one of his greatest triumphs.

The British striking force, including the company which Corporal Juma belonged, was concentrated in the forward areas preparatory to the advance on Italian Somaliland. Once day while on water fatigue at the River Tana, Juma fell into conversation with a Somali who spoke in the Swahili tongue.

He mentioned the fact that he had no great zest in drinking water.

"Across the river", said the Somali, "there is a hut ten miles away where you may taste very strong Somali liquor."

It was false information. Fanatical Mohammedans, the Somalis do not touch intoxicating drink. But Juma did not know that.

"Where is this hut?" he asked.

"If you meet me here at sunset the day after to-morrow I will lead you there."

Juma hesitated. The far bank of the river was out of bounds, and if discovered on that side he would get into serious trouble. But the chance to drink strong Somali liquor was an experience not to be missed – and besides, it would be at night. "Good, he said. "I will come."

So it happened that the day following the next Corporal Juma, his two brothers, his five cousins and a couple more Baganda compatriots volunteered for the evening water fatigue, and on arrival at the rendezvous hid their lorry in the bush. Their Somali guide was awaiting them.

Only one military policeman was on duty at the improvised bridge, and as he had to patrol as far as the improvised ferry fifty yards away, it was not difficult for the party to sneak across during his absence. On reaching the forbidden territory on the far side they set off at a resolute pace along a jungle path, and after about three hours arrived at a lone hut.

"This is the place", said their guide. "Go in and you will have some very strong liquor served to you."

They entered, to find the hut empty of all save a crude lamp tied to a pole in the centre and giving forth a fitful illumination.

"Where is the liquor?" demanded Juma.

"It is hidden in the bush. Wait while I fetch it."

They waited. When the Somali returned it was in the company of a dozen other Somalis, and these were all dressed in askari uniform and they all carried rifles.

Their uniforms were not as the uniforms of the British askari, their equipment was altogether dissimilar, and their rifles of quite a different pattern.

"What is this affair?" asked Juma. "Where is the liquor?"

"There is no liquor", replied the guide. "I am sergeant of the Banda and you are prisoners of the Italian Government."

The unarmed Baganda looked uneasily at the rifles and for once Juma's very quick wits did not misfire.

"Brother", he explained advancing with outstretched hands upon the man who had lured him into the trap. "This is indeed most astonishingly good fortune. Why I, the great Juma, and my kinsman have come all the way from Uganda to fight for the brave Italiani."

The Somali was taken aback.

"Is it true what this chief says" he asked, his eyes alighting on Matua.

"Truly", replied Matua gravely.

"Of course it is true", urged Juma. "Why, do you suppose that we noble Baganda would shed our blood on the same side as the Wakamba jackals!" And his spit bespoke so authentic an emotion that the Somali sergeant was convinced.

# X. EXPLOSION

Themselves masters of the art of dissimulation, it did not occur to the Somalis that the simple Bantus from the south were capable of duplicity, so that when their sergeant interpreted Juma's remarks they all beamed with pleasure and there followed much handshaking.

"Good!" said the sergeant. "Now we must set out for the frontier to report to our officer. The Italian bwanas will be very pleased, and you, O Juma, they will make a great man in their army."

Juma did not doubt that. He would be a great man wherever he went. Only he did not propose to go to the Italian frontier.

"Yes, we must make our journey", he said, "but first I must go back for all the other Baganda."

"All the other Baganda?"

"Yes, all the Baganda. There are thousands on the other side of the river waiting for the opportunity to fight for the Italiani. Is that not so, Matua?"

"Truly", said Matua.

The Somali sergeant pondered this proposition, but decided that one Baganda bird in the hand was worth thousands in the bush.

"No", he said. "We will come back for them some other time."

"Perhaps that would be better", agreed Juma, whose brain was working very well indeed. "How far do we need to travel?"

"It is three days' journey to the frontier."

"Three days!" exclaimed Juma. "That will never do. Know you not that I am a most important man in the army of the Inglesi, and if they found me missing they would sent out their iron birds to look for me, and those birds which see all things would discover our safari and drop their fierce eggs upon us?"

"Perhaps", said the sergeant. "But there is no other choice."

"Truly there is another choice", urged Juma. "Do you forget that we have a lorry hidden in the bush across the river and that there is only one man guarding the bridge?"

"That is so."

"Well, let us go softly to the bridge, creep upon the sentry and strangle him, and then all we have to do is get the lorry and I will drive you all to the frontier. Instead of three days safari we shall be able to report to your Bwana officer within three hours. Think how we shall spare our legs, and how pleased the Italiani will be to possess a good lorry in addition to our services."

The idea of being saved three days' foot-slogging made a great appeal to the Somalis.

"Yes", said their sergeant. "That is an excellent scheme. Come let us go to the bridge and strangle the sentry."

The mixed party of Somali and Baganda defiled along the bush path and made rapid progress in the moonlight. As they drew near the bridge Juma began to seek somewhat desperately for a plan of escape. But he need not have troubled himself. His lucky star was to take a hand in the game and decide the issue.

What Juma did not know was that they were not alone in their journey to the river. Less than a hundred yards in front of them was an elephant also on the move, intent on slaking his thirst.

And what the elephant in turn did not know was that the British bridge-head was guarded by land-mines. Had the elephant known this important fact he would doubtless have chosen some other route to the river, instead of which he trod upon a mine and transported himself in that second to fields of elephantine bliss.

The explosion was terrific. Somali and Bagandi threw themselves down upon the trembling ground while sand and gravel and bits of tree fell all around them. A huge missile came hurtling through the air and landed with a sickening "plump" between Juma and the Somali sergeant, making them both ill in the stomach.

It was the latter who first emerged from paralysis.

Believing that the British had spotted the party and brought their heaviest artillery to bear upon them, he turned to Juma for aid.

"Tell your gunners not to shoot any more, O Juma, for we cannot resist such terrific thunder. Tell your gunners not to shoot and we shall come as prisoners."

Awakening from his terror, Juma exploited the situation with a highly commendable presence of mind. Seeing the sergeant's rifle on the ground he leapt for it and then levelled it at his former captor.

"Instruct your Somalis to hand over their rifles to my Baganda", he ordered. The surrender was duly made. "That is good. If any dog of a Somali tries to escape he will be shot dead and our big guns will speak again and kill you all". They did as they were told.

In the excitement nobody stopped to examine the dread missile which had fallen between Juma and the Somali sergeant. Had this been done the missile would have been found to consist of the major portion of the hind-quarters of an elephant.

*" the explosion was terrific "*

# XI. EXAGGERATION

The British picquets in the bridge-head area were standing around the mine-crater and examining it with interest, thus leaving both the bridge and its approaches clear. Juma made a slight detour to reach the bridge without being seen and brought his party safely to the other side of the river. His mind was dancing with delight at the thought of the praises he would receive, but it did not on that account neglect certain practical considerations.

Thus he halted his prisoners before putting them on the lorry and addressed the Somali sergeant.

"Understand", he said. "There must be no mention made in this affair of our going to look for liquor."

"Truly", said the sergeant.

"It is for your own interest that I speak this. If my Bwana officer knew that you had led us into a trap he would take a tow-rope and hang you to a tall tree. You would not like that."

"Truly", agreed the sergeant, "I should not like that."

"Therefore whatever you hear me say to my Bwana officer you will declare on oath that it is true."

"I shall do that."

"Enough! Let us go forward." They scrambled into the vehicle.

When they arrived at camp they found the company awakened by the terrific explosion, standing-to in the moonlight.

Juma's Bwana officer looked with surprise as the party, having alighted, approached him. At this time his drivers had not been issued with arms, yet here were his Baganda all carrying rifles and escorting about a dozen men in strange uniforms.

"What is this affair?" he demanded.

"It is a very good affair, Effendi", replied Juma. "I have been in a big battle with the enemy and these are my prisoners."

"Indeed, and how did you manage to get into this battle?"

"I was at the river getting water, Effendi, when some men said there were thousands of Somali Banda coming to fight with our Askari. So I took my Baganda across the bridge and when we came upon the enemy's army we charged them and they turned and ran because our charge was too terrible to face. All except these men."

Juma indicated his prisoners. "These men stood and fought us, but we leapt upon them and tore their rifles out of their hands, and because they could not withstand our bravery they surrendered to us."

The officer contemplated him in silence, whereupon Juma shot a menacing glance at the Somali sergeant.

This gentleman, harbouring visions of a tow-rope on a tall tree, rushed in to confirm the story. "What this Baganda corporal has said is true, Effendi. He and his men charged upon us with such desperate courage that we put up our hands. I think this corporal is the bravest man in the world."

Juma heard this tribute with gratification. He then saw his officer's eyes were still upon him.

"That is the affair, Effendi."

"I see. And what was that very big noise across the river?"

"It was the noise of our great battle, Effendi", explained Juma, intent upon making all things serve his fame.

"That, clearly, is nonsense", said the officer. "I do not think this happened quite as you describe it."

"Indeed it did, Effendi", put in the obliging Somali sergeant.

"Silence! As I was saying Juma, I do not think that this affair was quite as you said. But it cannot be denied that you have brought in twelve prisoners and somehow or other managed to get hold of their rifles and that is very commendable. It is even possible that to do this thing you acted as a brave man. I will give you the benefit of the doubt. You will take these men to the police askaris and then report back to me."

Fifteen minutes later, the task completed, Juma reported back.

"Corporal Juma, I am sorry to say that Sergeant Kangata has been taken very ill."

"Good, Effendi", said Juma, with great sincerity.

"Nothing of the kind. Sergeant Kangata is a fine soldier and an excellent N.C.O. I shall miss him very much. However, as you have behaved very well for a long time now, I have decided to make you acting sergeant in his place."

"Oh thank you, Effendi; thank you, thank you very much indeed." He saluted three times in rapid succession to reinforce expression of his gratitude. "Oh thank you Effendi! Thank you."

"Just one more thing", said the officer. "I do not know what happened to-night, but if you really go out to fight the Banda remember next time that your business is to drive your lorry and not to look for battles. That is the affair of the infantry askari."

"Oh thank you, Effendi; thank you very much indeed."

He saluted again and went off, to find his brother waiting for him along the path.

He broke the great news about his promotion to Matua, who rejoiced.

"Indeed you should be made sergeant-major", he said, "so marvellously did you manage the affair tonight."

"Yes", Juma agreed. "I did manage the affair most marvellously. Those stupid dogs of Somalis thought I would fight for the Italiani." He spat into the moonlight. "Perhaps they thought I did not notice how the Italiani give them the tarbush to wear. Would I exchange my fine hat for a tarbush?"

"No, truly."

"Besides have I not made a promise to the King of the Inglesi?"

"Truly. And the King of the Inglesi will give you a great reward for you services to-night."

"Beyond doubt. Perhaps I shall myself be made a king."

Which was a happy thought with which to rock himself to sleep.

" *would I exchange my fine hat for a tarbush?* "

# XII. PREMONITION

Had Juma's fame not soared so high, then maybe his subsequent fortunes would not have fallen so low. Who can tell?

But soar it certainly did. The news of his exploit, as given in his own version, reached all the thousands of askari encamped by the river. And they marvelled to hear of it, and were exceedingly proud to have such a man among them.

Next day, too, an event took place which still further heightened his dramatic effect. A battalion of the Eritrean Labour Corps, which had been building a road beyond Tana, were passing back in lorries on the way to Nairobi, thence to join the Emperor Haile Selassie in the Sudan.

There was a general rush to see these grave, fuzzy headed men, who were very much like Somalis in appearance.

"Ow!" ran the murmur among the spectators. "Behold these hundreds upon hundreds of Banda! They are Juma's prisoners."

The great Sergeant Juma was there in person, watching the Fuzzies go by. He heard what was being said and he did not contradict it. He did not contradict it because he believed it with all the passionate conviction of his heart. Not for one moment did he doubt that these men were Italian Somali Banda, and that hearing of his terrific deeds the previous night, they had swarmed in to surrender lest they be called upon to fight so formidable and dread a warrior.

After the last lorry had gone past Juma turned and strode back to his lines, followed by askaris of every unit, anxious to feast their eyes upon this Baganda god. If there was a marked increase of importance in his stride – well, who would be so petty as to blame him for that? Not long afterwards, the great British advance upon Italian Somaliland started, with Sergeant Juma driving the first infantry-filled lorry behind his Bwana officer's car. They were in the vanguard of the column.

The infantry askari, normally looking down with contempt upon mere drivers, took up a different attitude in Juma's company. They felt flattered and privileged – and protected.

Another circumstance helped to crown his fame. In all the long and sweltering advance across the desert wastes to the Italian frontier no opposition whatever was encountered.

True, the British Intelligence Officers were well aware that no opposition was to be expected in this arid region, but the African askari were not to know that. They had imagined themselves pushing forward under constant fire every mile of the way, instead of which not a shot was fired.

There could only be one explanation of this miracle and they hastened to seize upon it. The Italian army, knowing Juma to be on the way, had fled before the thunder of his approach. So long as the Baganda god consented to remain with the column all would be well – a bloodless victory was assured.

Sergeant Juma heard this explanation and supported it. Clearly it was the truth.

After the third day's safari Juma and his favourite brother sat talking by the side of Juma's lorry.

"Consider, Matua", said Juma. "Consider how the battle I won that night we crossed the river has made all things easy for the Inglesi. There is such a fear for me in the hearts of the Italiani that they have all run away to their own country, and now the Inglesi will quickly conquer the land of the Somali and then the land of the Habashi. Does not the King of the Inglesi owe me a very great reward?"

"Truly", said Matua.

"I think I will ask the King of the Inglesi to give it to me at once."

"Truly", said Matua, and then as an afterthought: "But where is the King of England that you may ask him? Is he travelling with us in this column?"

"I do not think so", replied Juma.

There was silence while he pondered further upon this point, after which he announced with decision:

"No, certainly the King of the Inglesi is not in this column. Were he here he would have come to see me and brought me my reward with his own hands."

"Truly", said Matua, his sense of logic completely satisfied by the answer. It was irrefutable.

Then Matua had a brain-wave. "Since the King is not here, why do you not go and ask our Bwana officer about your reward?" was his suggestion.

Juma's face darkened. "I will tell you why, O Matua. It is because our Bwana officer is very jealous of me."

There was a silence, this time while Matua digested the issue raised.

"How can that be", he said at length. "Has he not just made you a sergeant?"

Juma could not deny that. "True!" he said.

"Besides", went on Matua, "your presence in his section makes him a very big man. Beyond doubt he boasts to all the other white men that he is the Bwana officer of the great Juma. Why then should he be jealous of you? I think he loves you as a brother."

This idea pleased Juma. The more he thought about it the more certain he became that Matua was right. Of course, under the circumstances, his Bwana officer could not fail to love him as a brother.

At that moment, in a distant part of the lines, his Bwana officer was remarking to the Bwana Mkubwa of the company:

"You know, sir, I have a hunch that I'm going to have some more trouble with that roaring scallywag Juma very soon."

There was no brotherly love in his tone, but it was not altogether lacking in affection.

# XIII. DISILLUSION

Juma's chance to broach the subject nearest to his heart soon came, for his Bwana officer's car temporarily broke down a couple of days later and after giving instructions for it to be towed in the rear of the company the Bwana officer took his place beside him in the lorry he was driving.

Juma beamed with delight, although he could scarcely fail to notice that his white superior was not in the same amiable frame of mind.

To tell the truth these were gruelling days for all of them. The sun imposed an insufferable tyranny on men foolish enough to travel in those forbidding regions. The sand blew up, blearing their eyes and begriming their mouths. The scene changed only so far as sparse shrub gave way to sparser shrub, and yellow soil to red soil and back again. The track became ever more impossible; vehicles were embedded axle-deep and had to be man-handled out by the infantry, only to sink again into the eroded earth a few years further on. There was little water.

But the worst plague of all was the sun.

Juma was mightily impressed by the toils exacted from him, quite apart from the impression made upon him by his own triumphs. He decided, therefore, to make his approach in general terms.

"Effendi", he began. "This is a very bad country."

There was no reply, as his Bwana had a distaste for the obvious.

"It does very bad things with all of us", he went on.

"What bad things?"

"Well, Effendi, the sun makes you white men go black and we black men go blacker."

"What of it?"

"Our women will not look with favour upon us if we return to them too black in the face."

"Not in my country", the white man mused grimly to himself. "There all handsome men are slightly sunburnt."

He happened to glance at his companion and noticed that the sand had pigmented him a bright yellow.

"At any rate you needn't worry for the time being old boy", he said. "At this moment you are so Nordic in colouring that you'd be accepted for Hitler's S.S."

"Effendi, I do not understand those words."

"Never mind, skip it", replied the officer, and lapsed into his former sultry silence.

But Juma was now thoroughly worked up to pursue his main point, though still in general terms. He came out with it pat.

"Effendi, what reward will we get for doing such hard work in this very bad country?"

"You'll get your pay."

Juma received this announcement without enthusiasm. "Will the Government not give us much land?" he asked.

"Where from?"

Juma considered the problem gravely. He solved it to his own entire satisfaction.

"Effendi, the Government could take away land from those who stay with their wives and give it to us that fight for the King of the Inglesi."

"I shouldn't bank on that if I were you", replied the officer.

"But, Effendi –"

The effendi, however, was sick of the subject.

"Bas", he said. "Enough."

Juma drove on with dismay in his soul until a bright thought occurred to him.

"I am a fool", he told himself solemnly. "Here am I pestering the Bwana officer about a thing too great for his decision. Only the King of the Inglesi is big enough to decide upon the reward I am to receive. And because my Bwana officer does not like to tell me that he is too small a man to name my reward – I hurt him in his pride by asking him about it. Yes, truly I am a fool."

He had just arrived at that satisfying conclusion when his Bwana officer sat up with a start. Following his gaze Juma saw stretching away north and south of the track a strip of sand entirely cleared of bush. In that flat land the eye could not see the end of it in either direction, even though it ran in a dead straight line. Thus did the Italians mark their frontiers.

When the lorry passed over it the Bwana officer turned to Juma and said, a note of elation in his voice:

"Juma, we are now in the territory of the Italiani."

For all men, especially those of an invading force, there is a thrill in crossing frontiers. Juma's heart, too, burst into song.

"So, Effendi", he replied, and added under his breath: "Thanks to me."

Poor Juma! At that moment a shot rang out. And then another. And another.

"Stop!" shouted the officer. The column came to an abrupt halt, and the infantry dismounted to deal with the situation, as was their function. Soon British askari, under their white officers, were deploying into the bush with rifles at the "ready".

Firing now broke out in real earnest. It was evident that both sides had joined battle. Machine-guns began to bark and bullets whistled over the lorries.

Poor Juma! He had been genuinely convinced that the advance had been unopposed because of the fame of his valour among the Italiani hosts, and that it would continue unopposed all the way to Addis Ababa and final victory. And yet here and now – it was unthinkable.

Unless – he leapt upon the idea – unless these particular troops did not know that he, Juma, was in the column. That must be it! Of course it was! He hastened to his officer.

"Effendi", he said. "These Italiani do not know I am here. Let me go where they are fighting so that I may call out to them: 'Ho! Italiani! Give me your rifles, for it is I, the great Juma, who speaks.'"

The officer's reply was not in of a nature to be printed. "Go back to your lorry", he added, "and be ready to move off in any direction I may say."

Juma obeyed. While the clatter of battle continued he sat glowering in his driver's seat, and there entered into his mind skirmishers of that dark mood of his which so soon were to bring his fortunes tumbling into the dust.

# XIV. HUMILIATION

The infantry beat back their attackers, pursued them some distance into the bush, and returned in high spirits to where their lorries awaited them. A rest for an hour was ordered for the mid-day meal, after which the second-in-command of the battalion came along to speak to Juma's Bwana officer.

"Look, old boy", he said. "We're going to push now for another twenty miles or so, except for one platoon which is to stay and have another crack at those blighters out there, and, if possible, rope in some prisoners. There may be an element of surprise, as the Itis, seeing the dust of our lorries, will think we have all moved on."

"Yes, sir", said Juma's Bwana officer.

"Well now, this is rather important," continued the Major. "The Colonel wants one of your lorries to wait here and pick up the platoon on its return."

"Yes, sir."

"So will you detail your most reliable driver for the job."

The M.T. Officer did some rapid thinking. As there was no Nubian gin for hundreds of miles around, Juma seemed the obvious selection. He was a superb driver, a useful mechanic, and a man of courage and resource.

"I would suggest Juma, sir – my African sergeant."

"Sergeant, eh! That sounds an excellent idea." Juma was called over.

"Listen, Sergeant", said the Major. "Your Bwana officer tells me that you are his best driver and a reliable N.C.O."

In an instant all Juma's sulks vanished and a broad smile of delight engulfed his features.

"Assahanti sana Effendi. Thank you. Thank you very much indeed."

"Now this is very important. In five minute the column goes forward – every lorry except one. Your lorry stays here. You stay here until a platoon comes to find you – perhaps in two hours time. Do you understand?"

"Yes, Effendi."

"Then repeat what I have said."

"All the garis are going, Effendi, but my gari stays here. I wait until the infantry askari come."

"Good. You will not forget?"

"Effendi, I will not forget."

Satisfied, the Major went and reported to the Colonel. Soon after, a whistle blew and lorries in unending succession pulled out and passed the lorry in which Juma sat exalted.

He paid no attention to them, for joy was diffused throughout his whole being.

It was now clear that his Bwana officer had meant none of the outrageous things he had said to him an hour ago. Had he not just sung his praises to the Bwana major? Had he not just been picked for a job of the utmost importance and hazard. Did it not mean that he was destined to climb to the very pinnacle of military glory?

Assuredly.

The question of that reward was again placed beyond doubt. More, as a result of this vital task entrusted to him by the Bwana major it would be multiplied a thousand-fold.

There had once been two Kings of Uganda: why could there not be two Kings of the Inglesi, King Georgi and King Juma. It might well happen. After all, the means to repay supreme services were limited. King Georgi was not the potentate to give his noblest servants less than they deserved.

Clearly, then, he would become joint King of England. It was as good as settled.

He would sail across the sea in a huge ship, and that ship would be filled with his wives – thousands and thousands of them. He would have every woman in Uganda sent to him for inspection.

Which of those that he knew already would he choose?

It was a gorgeous happiness selecting them thus in advance. Juma spent perhaps an hour thereon, when suddenly he awoke to the realities about him. He was horrified to find himself alone in the midst of overwhelming silence. The column must have moved on leaving him – asleep! Whatever would his Bwana officer say when he discovered that the great Juma was absent. And through such a cause! Ow! This was a very bad affair.

With panic in his heart and fingers he pressed the self-starter, accelerated and shot-forward along the track at an ever more desperate speed.

Juma drove like a man possessed. He had but one thought in his head – to catch up with the column and stave off the wrath to come.

After half an hour's demon-driving he saw smoke arising from innumerable fires ahead of him and knew that he had arrived at the bivouac for the night.

A group of officers were standing on the right of the track – the Infantry Major, his own Bwana Mkubwa and his own Bwana officer. Juma halted and jumped down, saluting with an enormous, knowing grin on his face, as though to say "Ah! You thought you left me behind, but you didn't know your Juma."

The Infantry Major saw red. His colonel had entrusted him with the laying-on of this lorry. And it was no mere battalion matter either. The Brigadier himself had given orders for that platoon, now so maddeningly left behind. The Major felt himself blindingly, helplessly let down.

"What's happened?" he snapped.

"I had engine trouble, Effendi, but I soon put it right and now I am here." His grin was more expansive than ever as he thought of how clever he had been in putting right the engine-trouble that had never existed.

An overwhelming urge came over the Major – at all costs to take that fatuous grin off the maniac's face. He lunged forward.

Juma picked himself up with the entire bottom knocked out of his world. Not until that instant did he remember his implicit instructions to stay for the infantry platoon.

The Colonel strode upon the scene. "What's all this?" he demanded. The Major explained, whereupon the Colonel turned to Juma's Bwana officer.

"Just like these blasted M.T. Outfits", he snarled. "Utterly unreliable."

The Bwana officer thus addressed pulled himself up.

*" with an enormous knowing grin "*

"You've had good service from us until this incident, sir," he replied. He gave the Colonel a somewhat vehement salute, and before any retort could be forthcoming he had jumped into the driving seat of Juma's lorry, reversed the vehicle, and gone roaring back along the track to do the job that Juma had left undone.

Although he understood no English, Juma knew that he had got his Bwana officer into trouble. He slunk away with a heavy heart.

## XV. INTOXICATION

If Juma had made good time in catching up with the column, it was nothing to the speed with which his officer hurtled on the way back. It was a fantastic speed, dictated not only by the desire to put right what had gone so grievously wrong, but by a good healthy rage as well.

Not so much rage over Juma's folly. Juma was like most Africans – the more towering their virtues the more staggering their defects and the more inexplicable the occasions on which these defects were manifested.

But rage over that disgusting jibe of the Colonel's. The swine must have known very well that everything else we've done for him has gone like clock-work, he brooded.

He, too, fell into a day-dream as the machine raced along the track, although it was a very different day-dream from Juma's. He visualised a miraculous change of fortune wherein the position of subaltern and colonel were reversed and he was sitting in judgement on that pompous ass with his silly, swaggering moustachios. He began to devise ingenious sneers and indignities, until his common-sense asserted itself.

"Snap out of it!" he said to himself. "What the hell's the use of cluttering up your mind with tripe like that!"

An Italian patrol in the bush helped him out of his mood. A bullet fired at an oblique angle smashed his wind-screen and sent fragments of glass hurtling into his face.

The track chose this moment to give way, so that the vehicle sank deep into the sand. With a curse he put the gears into reverse, and managing with great good luck to get clear, he made a detour round the soft patch and raced forward again while bullets ripped into the woodwork of the cab and bodywork.

In a short time he had driven out of range and not long afterwards he came across the platoon, which finding no lorry, had begun to march. The platoon had captured an Italian officer and four Eritrean askaris and were in grand fettle.

After seeing everybody aboard, its young commander climbed cheerfully into the seat beside the M.T. officer.

He looked with astonishment at the smashed wind-screen, and then saw that his companion's face was streaming with blood from innumerable cuts.

"Hallo, hallo, old boy, what's happened to you?" he asked.

"Mosquitoes", growled the other. "You'd better warn your fellows at the back to have their rifles ready, as we may run into them again on the way back."

But the return journey was uneventful. They drove up to the Battalion Headquarters, where the Colonel came out to watch them alight. His face lit up when he saw the prisoners.

"Well done, Brown", he said to his subaltern. Then he turned to the M.T. officer who had not dismounted from his seat.

"Lucky for you! I was going to place you under arrest, but you've just managed to save your bacon."

The M.T. officer made no reply, but drove off to rejoin his section. Walking down the lines a moment later he saw Juma squatting in earnest conversation with Matua. Here was the cause of the whole damned affair. His boot itched. But when he saw the expression on

Juma's face he passed on without saying a word. He reached his own company's headquarters.

"Hallo" said his Company Commander. "Been starting a private war of your own?"

"I'd like to start one with that ruddy colonel." He gave a brief account of what had happened as he stood in front of a piece of looking-glass and dabbed his cuts with iodine.

"That's nothing", said the Company Commander. "After you'd gone he even threatened to put me under arrest for what he described as your dumb insolence."

Both of them had to laugh.

"What about your precious Juma?" asked the Bwana Mkubwa. "Are you going to bring a charge against him?"

"I don't think so, sir," replied the other. "What's the blasted use? God alone knows what bug bit him, but I'm quite sure that he did not deliberately disobey orders. Besides, if we took away his stripes it would only be a matter of time before the man we promoted in his place became equally eccentric."

"Very likely" said the Bwana Mkubwa, who knew his Africa. "Have a drink."

Meanwhile a most unfortunate thing was happening in the lines. A convoy had just driven in with a company of the infantry battalion which had been left behind as reserve on the River Tana. And Juma, who had watched them arrive, found among them a bosom friend of his from Uganda. He took him over to his Baganda group by the lorries, where there was much hand shaking prior to sitting down in a circle and exchanging news.

"I have heard much about you, O Juma", said the newcomer. "You are now a very great man."

"Yes" agreed Juma, though without his usual assurance, for he was still feeling exceedingly sheepish.

"Your fame has already reached Nairobi. In a few days it will reach Uganda. In a week it will be all over the world."

"Truly", said Juma. His voice remained subdued.

And then the other took from his pocket a commodity they had not seen for weeks – the beautiful, intoxicating drug called bhang.

An hour later Juma was recounting how, when left alone that afternoon, the whole Italian army had attacked his lorry, and how he had driven them all off by leaning through the window of his cab and calling out in a voice of thunder:

"Beware! I am the great Juma."

"They made a great dust as they ran away", he added reminiscently.

# XVI.  INTIMIDATION

Now one of the troubles of bhang is that it makes thirsty the throats of those who use it. Indeed, not only does it induce thirst, but a certain irresponsibility as to ways and means whereby that thirst may best be quenched.

Sergeant Juma was travelling in a parched desert where water had to be brought hundreds of miles from the river, and to emphasise its value his Bwana officers throughout this period even went without shaves. On each lorry a reserve of twelve gallons was carried, but the threats as to what would happen if this reserve was touched made the drivers think twice before stealing a single sip.

Until the fumes of bhang had entered his head Juma, too, had a proper attitude towards this matter, but after a few whiffs he soared into a dream world where no threats were valid and where the only realities were his own desires.

Matua notice that his brother was going rather strong on the water and mentioned it. "Will not the Bwana officer be very angry?" he asked.

"The Bwana is my brother", replied Juma. "Besides, if there is any affair I will make a great magic and cause a river to flow besides the track, so that all may drink and the Bwana once more will be able to cut the hairs off his face. That will please him."

"Truly", said Matua, well content.

On the evening of the following day Bwana Sergeant Robinson came round the lines. Juma, for all his newly-claimed magicianship, was little disquieted to find that the white man came with the sole intention of checking the water reserves.

Every driver was allowed two gallons leakage: more than that constituted an entry in the sergeant's notebook and subsequent punishment. But the only excess was that of Matua, who emboldened by his brother's promise of magical intervention had got through four gallons. His name was taken.

The Bwana sergeant was about to go off when a thought struck him.

"Perhaps while I am here Sergeant Juma, I'd better give your water-debis the once over – just to do the job thoroughly.

"Yes, Effendi. You will find all my water in the debis."

The white sergeant went up to shake a tin, more as a matter of form than anything else. It yielded a negative result. So did all the other tins. Juma was twelve gallons short – his entire reserve.

Sergeant Robinson looked puzzled. "What's the idea, Sergeant Juma?"

"This is lion-country, Effendi. I think the lions have drunk my water."

"That's very interesting", replied Sergeant Robinson. "Get hold of the lions at once and bring them up before the Bwana Mkubwa for punishment. That will let you out. Meanwhile you are under arrest."

He went off, leaving Juma with murder in his eyes.

"Do not be angry, O Juma," said his brother. "Make your magic river and bring the affair of the water to an end."

Juma looked gloomily at Matua. "That is foolish talk", he said. "Do you think I will trouble to make a big magic for the benefit of white men who spy upon me – me, the great Juma? Let them die of thirst." And he spat one of his most savage spits.

The report was duly made.

"This is beyond a joke", said Juma's Bwana officer with a groan. "What do you propose this time?" asked the Bwana Mkubwa. "Let it go again?"

"No, sir. Hang it all, how can I? There must be some discipline. We can't have everybody drinking up his reserves or the company will die of thirst."

"The same answer holds good as on the previous occasion", grunted the Bwana Mkubwa. "We can only demote him, and the lunatic we put in his place will very likely do something even more damned silly."

"I can't help that, sir. Useful N.C.O. though he is, his stripes will have to come off. That is, if you're willing to do it."

"It's your affair and I'll do what you wish", said the Company Commander. "That goes without saying. Meanwhile there are a couple of tots left in the whisky bottle. Let's have them before your voracious sergeant sniffs them out."

"Not yet, if you don't mind", replied Juma's Bwana officer. "First I'll have to try and scrounge twelve gallons of water from the South Africans to make good the loss. When that unsavoury job's over I'll come back and drink to the damnation of all Africa." He went off to his car and drove off.

Juma's Baganda followers had gathered about him. They wanted to know what he would say to the Bwana Mkubwa when he appeared in front of him.

"Oh" said Juma. "I'll make a very strong talk with the Bwana Mkubwa. I'll tell him that the British Government owes me twelve hundred wives and not just twelve gallons of water. I'll tell him that the King of the Inglesi will cut off his head if he makes an affair where there is no affair."

His followers gasped with amazement and were filled with renewed pride in their leader.

"Truly", said Matua, "I think that the Bwana Mkubwa will be greatly frightened."

# XVII. DEMOTION

When the time came for Juma to go in front of his Bwana Mkubwa his assurance had considerably evaporated. He therefore took a large dose of bhang to help him over the ordeal. Its effect was to make him, not aggressive and intimidatory, but full of love for all the world.

He stood smiling when the charge was read out to him. He beamed when the Bwana sergeant gave his evidence. And when asked what he had to say for himself he answered with the air of a man called upon to give a genial after-dinner speech.

"Effendi, this is not my affair" he said chuckling. "It is the affair of the Bwana sergeant. The Bwana sergeant likes affairs about water."

"Indeed!" said the Bwana Mkubwa. "I thought you told the Bwana sergeant that it was the affair of the lions."

In his mood of gay goodwill he did not wish to put all the blame on either party.

"Yes, Effendi", he said. "It is the affair of the Bwana sergeant and the lions."

"Are you mad?"

"Yes, Effendi. Thank you, I am very mad"

The Bwana Mkubwa looked over his shoulder to where Juma's Bwana officer was standing.

"Has this fellow been drinking?" he enquired.

"No, sir. I suspect bhang."

"Do you take bhang?" Juma was asked.

Juma was delighted. He thought he was being invited to a social occasion.

"Thank you, Effendi. If you have a cigarette I would prefer that."

The Bwana Mkubwa did not take the remark very well. When he had done commenting on it and on Juma himself – in language which won Juma's enthusiastic admiration – he delivered his judgement.

"Juma", he said. "I take away your stripes."

"Oh thank you, Effendi."

"You are no longer a sergeant."

"Good, Effendi. Thank you. I like not to be a sergeant."

"Of course you lose your sergeant's pay."

"I am glad, Effendi. Thank you very much indeed."

"Reversion to the ranks", snapped the Bwana Mkubwa. The Bwana sergeant major repeated the sentence, and Driver Juma was marched off with a look of ecstasy on his face, as though he had been admitted into Paradise.

"You know", said Bwana Mkubwa to Juma's Bwana officer, "I am sure the blighter's cracked."

"Bhang, sir" replied the other. "I recognise the symptoms. He won't be so happy about things when the effects wear off. We shall be in for some more trouble then if I know anything about it."
Fifty yards away the Bwana sergeant major produced a knife and cut the three stripes off each of Juma's arms.

Juma submitted, enraptured. He clapped his hands with joy when the operation was done. "Thank you very much, Effendi", he said.

On his return to the lines his friends looked with horror upon his stripe-less sleeves.

"This is a very bad thing that the Bwana Mkubwa has done to you", they said.

Juma bestowed a beautiful smile upon them. "The Bwana Mkubwa would not do a very bad thing to me. He is my brother."

"But your stripes. He has taken away your stripes."

"True", agreed Juma. "But why has he done that? I will tell you. He has taken away my stripes to-day so that to-morrow he may place a crown in their place. He has taken away my hundred shillingi a month so that to-morrow he may pay me one hundred thousand shillingi a month."

The Baganda drivers were dumbfounded. "A crown! A hundred thousand shillingi a month!"

When they had recovered they shook him by the hand with shouts of glee. Juma decided that he liked hand-shaking. He shook their hands in return, went over to the contemptible Wakamba and shook their hands, and then strode over to the infantry lines and shook the hands of six hundred startled infantry askaris.

When there were no more hands to be shaken he crawled under his lorry to sleep it off.

"You know, sir", his Bwana Officer was saying to the Bwana Mkubwa, "before coming out here I imagined that neurosis was a disease of civilisation."
"Well?"

"Well, it just isn't. These blighters of ours are neurotics. Take Juma for instance –"

"Juma's a howling maniac."

"No, I don't agree with you there, sir. But he's as neurotic as you make them. Damned pathetic, really."

"I could find another word for it", said the Bwana Mkubwa, who had no urge to delve into the mystery of Juma's soul.

At that moment there was a wild shriek. A scorpion, it appears, had crowned an adventurous journey along one of the legs of the sleeping Juma by stinging him on the seat.

The two officers jumped up and saw the wretched victim running round in desperate circles clutching his injured part.

"There you are", growled the Bwana Mkubwa. "Didn't I tell you the man's a raving lunatic."

Juma's Bwana officer went to investigate. When he found out what was wrong he had him conducted to the medical post and returned to the Bwana Mkubwa.

"Scorpion bite, sir", he reported.

The Bwana Mkubwa was delighted. "Splendid!" he said. "Get me the scorpion's name and I'll put it up for the O.B.E."

## XVIII. ABERRATION


Next morning Juma woke up intolerably sore at both ends. But his physical soreness was nothing to his spiritual agony when he looked down at his sleeves and saw the three proud stripes no longer there. Recollection of the previous day's happenings began to bite into his consciousness and each was worse than the scorpion's sting.

Then Oparo, fat blundering Kamba Corporal, began to stride down the lines shouting out in a newly important voice: "All drivers fill up with petrol and water."

Juma gazed with horror at Oparo's sleeves. They contained the three glorious stripes which had been ripped from his own arms. Ow! Whom should he murder? This Kamba upstart, certainly. And the Bwana sergeant who had made out of the water an affair that was no affair. Like all Africans, Juma's rage was never against the man who punished him, but always against the informer.

"Hurry, Juma!" said the new sergeant. "We go soon."

Perhaps it would be better, he reflected, to obey the order of this Kamba pig first and do the murdering at some more opportune time. Juma went to his lorry in a towering fury.

"What an affair!" he muttered to himself. "If I had drunk twelve gallons of the white men's whisky they could not have made a bigger affair."

He took out the twelve gallons of water with which his Bwana officer had with great difficulty replaced his vanished reserves. So preoccupied was he with his own anger that he did not notice that he poured them – all twelve gallons – into his petrol tank.

That done, he took off the radiator-cap and poured petrol into his radiator. He was surprised that his engine failed to start.

When the time came to move off the infantry vanguard whom he normally carried had to climb into another lorry, while he was assigned to the rearguard, which would give his Bwana sergeant time to find out what had gone wrong and put it right. The whistle blew and off went the column.

After ten minutes of puzzled inspection Bwana Sergeant Robinson cleared up the mystery.

"Who filled your petrol tank this morning, Juma?" he asked. "You – or the lions?"

Eventually the matter was rectified and a sullen Juma prepared to drive off with the rearguard. Remembering that he still had some bhang left he regaled himself with a dose to restore his equanimity, for he was rightly proud of his powers as a driver and this ridiculous mistake had made him feel a fool.

The bhang soon put that right, though with still more disastrous consequences. He had gone about five miles when realisation came to him that he was no longer in his old honoured place at the head of the column. He brooded upon the fact while the fumes of bhang were wafted into his head.

"Ow!" he said to himself. "What is this new affair! Do they expect the most important man in the army to drive at the back, behind all the Wakamba jackals! It is a very bad affair, not to be endured."

Whereupon he pulled out, dashed his foot on the accelerator and at seventy miles an hour passed one hundred and seventy vehicles, to pull in again, triumphant, behind his Bwana officer's car at the head of the advance.

The rearguard had banged upon his cab to try and stop his mad career. He did not hear their banging. Drivers and infantry yelled at him all along the route. He thought they were yelling to encourage him. Halfway up the column the Infantry Colonel and his own Bwana Mkubwa shouted to him. He smiled a comradely smile and increased his speed.

Both the Colonel and his Bwana Mkubwa pulled out to chase him. This was a glorious excitement.

Drawing abreast of Juma's own Bwana officer's car in the very front the Colonel ordered the column to halt. Then he got out in a terrific frenzy.

"Have you no control over your blasted men?" he roared at the M.T. subaltern, who being in front had no idea what all the fuss was about.

The M.T. Bwana Mkubwa explained. "Our friend Juma again. He's just roared past the whole column at about a hundred miles an hour."

Juma's Bwana officer looked round and saw the culprit grinning amiably at him through the wind-screen.

"And now my rearguard has become my advance guard", blazed the Colonel, his military mind appalled by such disorderly proceedings. "I'll have you court-martialled for this."

"Thank you, sir. I should welcome a court-martial", replied Juma's Bwana officer, looking the Colonel straight in the eyes.

"He doesn't mean it", said the Bwana Mkubwa, when the irate Colonel had taken himself off.

"I wish to God he did", replied the subaltern. "I'd enjoy asking him in front of a court-martial if he had prophetic knowledge of the crazy urges of every askari under his command."

"What about Juma's crazy urges?"

"I suppose I ought to apply for the kiboko. But whipping won't help Juma, I'm afraid. What a life!"

A spare driver having been detailed to drive Juma's lorry, the column moved off again.

Juma sat with Matua.

"That was a wonderful speed you made", said Matua.

"Yes", agreed Juma. "But I think the Bwana Colonel is very angry because I make a bigger speed than he can make."

# IXX. EXECRATION


When Juma appeared for the second time in front of his Bwana Mkubwa he had no bhang left to soften the harsh lines of reality. He stood morosely to attention while evidence was given of the water in his petrol tank, and of the petrol found in his radiator. His expression did not change when it was related how he had broken his place in the column and careered like a madman to the front. He asked no questions, disputed no facts, said no word in defence. The skirmishers of his black mood had beckoned to the main body and the whole soul was now in their possession.

"Fourteen days field punishment on each count, making twenty-eight days in all", snapped the Bwana Mkubwa.

Juma returned to the lines, but gave no answer to the queries of his friends. When Matua followed for a sympathetic talk about the affair he was roughly pushed aside. Like Timon of Athens, Juma hated mankind.

The advance continued, sometimes without lights in the night, at other times in the sweltering heat of the day. Deprived of his vehicle, Juma sat as a spare driver beside Matua and never said a word. If anything went wrong with the lorry he did nothing to put it right. He left Matua and everybody else, including the King of the Inglesi, to stew in their own juice.

When the River Juba was reached and the fierce battle of Bulo Erillo took place, in which a Gold Coast regiment lost nearly all its gallant white officers, he suspected the reason to be that the Italiani, hearing of his disaffection, had found the heart to resist the British advance. So be it. Let the Inglesi take the consequences of having made him their enemy. But the thought brought him no joy and he still said no word.

Then the column drove thirty miles up the river, made a surprise crossing, and struck off through the unchartered jungle with a tank bull-dozing a track for the lorries. For three days they travailed thus, at an average speed of two miles an hour, before bursting forth upon the Jelib-Mogadishu road, thereby cutting off the retreat of the Italians defending the line of the Juba. This made Juma's black mood blacker. Was his disaffection to bring no disaster to British arms after all? It was a hideous thought.

Began the race to Mogadishu. For the first time in the campaign the road was good, and although vision was still restricted by the eternal bush, everybody in the column felt a sense of the poetry of motion and the grandeur of conquest as the engines purred rapturously towards the capture of the Italian capital. Everybody except Juma. Juma's soul was made sick by this easy progress for the Inglesi. His gods had all deserted him and he looked everywhere in vain for a prop with which to sustain his self-esteem.

One evening a wonderful thing happened. After being imprisoned for so long in the heart-breaking bush the column purred over pink sand-hills, in the glow of a pink sunset, and found the Indian Ocean at its feet. There was triumph in the sight.

None of the drivers had ever seen the sea, so after the infantry had been debussed, and a bivouac site selected, their Bwana officer took them down to the shore. They were almost hysterical with excitement, laughing and chattering like a bevy of schoolgirls in the presence of their favourite film star. When a wave approached they ran back with cries of alarm; when it receded they crept cautiously forward, only to repeat the process over and over again.

"Off with your clothes", said the Bwana officer, "We'll have a bathe in the sea."

"Effendi!" they gasped. "We fear the crocodiles."

"Nonsense", he replied laughing. "There are no crocodiles here", and taking off his own clothes he dashed into the water. Seeing that no misfortune befell their officer one by one the drivers followed his example, much to his delight. He felt that in addition to getting clean himself, he had – by enticing his followers into the sea – done his own nose a very good turn.

Splashing about in the water he looked back to the shore and saw that only two drivers had stayed behind – Juma and Matua.

"Come along, Matua", he called gaily, and that gentleman obeyed with a will.

Juma's black heart raged. "Am I the man to be thus ignored!" he snarled to himself. But he remained standing on the marge.

He looked upon the figures splashing in the water, with contempt, and upon the Indian Ocean with a hatred which suggested that he had added it to his black list as a thing to be murdered at the earliest possible date.

# XX. EXTEMPORISATION

Although he scorned to bathe in the sea, Juma saw no reason why he should not be allowed a few days in which to lie at peace upon the shore, and enjoy the breezes, and recuperate after the toils of the preceding months. But the authorities had other views. During the next two days the M.T. Company was early astir and driving into the sweltering interior to fetch successive batches of prisoners, after which Juma was obliged to parade on his own under the detested Sergeant Oparo, and do an hour's daily punishment drill on the sands.

He was marched and turned this way and that and doubled round in circles. He was halted and moved on. He was made to double mark-time. He was ordered to raise himself up and down on his hands and then turn over to wave his legs in the air. There was no end to the indignity heaped upon him. Although a rage smouldered in his heart, the figure he cut was infinitely pathetic.

On the second evening the Bwana office passed as Juma was being put through his paces. "Why does he come this way?" the panting defaulter asked himself, and promptly answered his own question. "The reason is clear: he comes that he may gloat upon me and take pleasure in my punishment."

In truth, after one glance, Juma's officer had turned his eyes away. "Poor devil!" he muttered to himself, and then again in the plural. "Poor devils!"

Perhaps he was including the whole of mankind. He was a queer bird, that officer.

After his dismissal Juma went and sat apart upon a sand-dune, and there a thought came to him. Why should he put up with this insufferable treatment when all he had to do was declare that he was sick? The question being – as far as he could see – unanswerable, he forthwith became a sick man and returned to the lines with the air of one about to die.

In the morning the company paraded according to custom.

"It is reported to me that you are sick. Is that so, Juma?" asked his officer.

"Yes Effendi."

"Then you may fall out and stay here all day."

Juma experienced his first feeling of delight for many a day. What a marvellous piece of malingering he had achieved! Truly the white men were no match for him in cleverness. While the others drove off to work through the heat he would seek a pleasant place and sleep.

But he had not hobbled very far from the parade when he became aware that all was not as usual. The drivers were not being marched to their vehicles: instead two lorries only were brought along, and into these all the other drivers crowded. Mogadishu had fallen to British arms, the Bwana officer had wangled a treat for his men by securing permission for them to spend a day in the Somaliland capital.

It was a terrific day. Left to their own devices on arrival, the drivers had formed up in threes and staged their own march through the streets, each man assuming the royal stride of a conqueror. After that they fell in with Arabs who sold them some pleasant intoxicant which warmed their hearts without destroying their brains. And the unbelievably beautiful Somali ladies smiled dazzling smiles at them. Conquerors they were, indeed!

*" Conquerors they were indeed ! "*

Finally they kept faith with their officer by returning to their lorries at the stipulated hour in the evening and were driven back to camp singing songs of the glory and grandeur of life.

Juma stood watching them as they arrived. Matua soon told him what had happened, and at once all his self-satisfaction oozed away from him. He looked out upon the sea with the eyes of a man who believes that it is his eternal lot to be defrauded and frustrated. But of one thing he was certain – he would not allow himself to be cheated when the splendid adventure was repeated next day.

"Still sick, Juma?" enquired his officer on the morning parade.

"No, Effendi, My sickness has gone."

"Good. Sergeant Oparo, march the section off to the lorries for prisoner of war fatigues."

So Juma was marched off with the rest, and he felt his stature to have dwindled beneath that of the simplest fool.

After the long day's work was done orders were given for the section to pack up and move off at once. The Italians were running as fast as they could go into the Abyssinian fastnesses and the British had set forth upon the chase. It was now to be the duty of the section to which Juma belonged to carry ammunition behind the foremost brigade.

That night it camped all on its own, fifty miles from the nearest unit.

"We shall have to find our own guard to-night, Sergeant Oparo", said the officer. "Take the spare drivers for the purpose. They can have my watch, but you will have to explain to each man where the hands must rest before he wakes up his relief."

"Yes, Effendi, I shall do that", replied the Wakamba sergeant.

Being now relegated to the despised position of spare driver Juma found himself selected as one of the guard.

When his turn came as sentry he stood where he had been told to stand, and to avoid boredom began to examine the Bwana officer's watch in the light of the moon. It was not long before he discovered that the moving of the hand was not the monopoly of the god within, but could also be managed through human agency. A great discovery, for who would be so idiotic as to stand for two hours among the jackals in the bush, when by pressing a knob and a twist of the fingers, the watch could be induced to annihilate those two hours, thus enabling the next man to be called instantly and the manipulator to return to his rest?

Certainly not Juma.

# XXI. SANITATION

When on lone convoy with his section the Bwana officer always made it a rule to start off at 4.30. This meant half-an-hour's driving in the dark and several hours in the comparative cool of the early morning, so that by breakfast the back of the safari had been broken and the rest of the day could be taken more easily.

At a quarter to four the last sentry would wake the Bwana sergeant and the Bwana sergeant in turn would wake the Bwana officer, and everything would be ready for a punctual start.

On this occasion the officer drove at the head of his column for half an hour before noting with surprise that there was no sign of dawn. He looked at his watch – now, of course restored to him – and wondered what had happened to the sun. Thereafter his incredulity increased with the minutes. At the end of another hour they were still driving through the night. Half an hour later the officer wondered in blank dismay whether there had been a cosmic accident which was to rob men forever of the light of the sun. And then, most tardily, there came the dawn – nearly two hours late.

When the convoy had halted for breakfast a white dispatch rider passed by and enabled the officer to check the time – his watch was an hour and three-quarters fast. And he knew his watch better than that. As he ate his breakfast of bully and biscuits his face wore a puzzled frown.

Then he called Sergeant Oparo. "Sergeant", he said. "Somebody on guard last night must have been tampering with my watch." He indicated the process whereby the hands could be moved at will. "Who could it have been?"

"I do not know, Effendi", replied the sergeant, but he proceeded to have a very good guess. "The next time Juma is on guard, Effendi, I will stay up myself to see what happens."

But Sergeant Oparo was wrong. There was to be no next time, for his own fortunes were on the verge of catastrophe, though he knew it not, whilst those of Juma were ready for another leap. It is well that men cannot see into the future.

Juma's fortunes began to mend that very evening, when the convoy caught up with the brigade in front and received orders to go into bivouac near at hand.

This enforced stay had not been foreseen, and it created a crisis, for it meant that refuse-pits would have to be dug, and the section, being on detachment, had no sweepers to attend to this little matter.

Bwana Sergeant Robinson detailed a Wakamba party to act as sweepers for the occasion. Soon afterwards the Bwana officer heard noises in the distance, and these became a hullabaloo as all the Wakamba in the section came swarming over to interview him. At their head, acting as their spokesman, was Sergeant Oparo.

"Effendi", he said. "The Bwana Sergeant has detailed eight Wakamba to dig choos."

"Well?"

"Effendi, it is not the custom of the Wakamba to do that thing."

"Is it the custom of the Wakamba to die of disease?"

"No, Effendi, but it is not our custom to dig choos."

"Why not?"

"Because it interferes with our marriage prospects."

Here was a pretty problem. Native superstition on the one hand; army discipline and hygiene on the other. The officer remembered the Indian Mutiny.

"What do you propose then? The choos must be dug."

"Yes, Effendi", agreed Sergeant Oparo. "But the Baganda can dig them."

"Why should the Baganda do fatigues for the Wakamba? Do their marriage prospects not matter?"

"Effendi, in this business their belief is different from ours."

"I still don't see why they should do your fatigues."

There was a murmur of assent from the Baganda who has begun to gather round.

"Listen, Sergeant Oparo", said the officer. "I do not wish to interfere with your customs and in future I will bring Kikuyu sweepers on safari, for it is their pleasure to dig choos for everybody. But in the meantime army orders must be obeyed and the health of askaris safeguarded. Those pits must be dug before dawn. Enough."

The drivers drifted back to their lines in silence, but once there agitated debate broke out and continued until the Bwana sergeant went over to stop the noise. A decision however had been arrived at by the Wakamba. It was that on no account would they dig those choos. They went to sleep instead.

"What is this affair?" asked Juma of his brother, for he had been at the infantry lines while the interview was taking place.

Matua told him, whereupon Juma turned over to go to sleep as well. But he soon woke up again. Some feeling stirred within him for which he could not account. Perhaps in the dim recesses of his soul he knew that for all the trouble there had been between them, the Bwana officer was his brother still.

It cost an effort, but he made it. "Come, wake all the Baganda", he said to Matua.

And for several hours the steady sound of Baganda picks and shovels digging the ground mingled with the hyaenas' cries while all else slept.

## XXII. CASTIGATION

During the morning Juma was summoned by his officer.

"Oh Juma", said the latter. "About the affair of the choos, I want to thank you."

For the first time since the disastrous affair of the water, away beyond the Juba, Juma beamed upon his Bwana.

"What you did was a big help to me in a difficult situation", continued the officer.

"Thank you Effendi, thank you very much indeed", replied Juma.

"You will be a spare driver no longer. You can go back to your own lorry.

Juma's spirits soared.

"Oh thank you, Effendi, that is very good. Thank you! Thank you!" Every "thank you" was accompanied by a luscious salute.

Driver Juma had set foot on the lowest rung in the ladder of his rehabilitation. He strode back exalted to the lines.

"Everything is now well" he told Matua. "The Bwana officer is very sorry about the way he treated me. 'Juma', he said to me 'my heart is sore because of what has been done to you. It was all the fault of the Bwana sergeant who made an affair where there was no affair. We will forget the bitterness about the water and be brothers again. You can once more drive your own gari, and as soon as possible I shall cast out the jackal Oparo into the dust and give you back your stripes.' Is that not good?"

"Truly", exclaimed the delighted Matua, "it is very good. And now the Inglesi will remember our battle of the river and consider the affair of the reward."

Juma agreed "Yes", he said, "the Bwana officer mentioned that."

In the afternoon Brigade gave orders for the M.T. section to hand over its ammunition load and return to the coast for more. Simultaneously the brigade pushed forward and sped so fast and so far into Abyssinia that Juma's officer on re-loading was staggered to learn that his convoy would have to carry its own petrol, food and water for twelve hundred miles.

"By Jove", he said to the Bwana sergeant. "This is going to be some safari."

It was.

The road as far as the Abyssinian frontier was excellent. "The Imperial Road to the Ocean", the Italians had named it. As the convoy sped along the hard surface the convoy commander purred with content. Here they were, going adventurously forth on their own into the blue, with no infantry colonels to worry them and no M.T. bureaucrats to call for petrol and oil returns. It was Heaven. Days, and perhaps weeks of perfect peace lay ahead of them, he reflected, and the desert would blossom like the rose in their especial honour. All of which went to show that Juma was not the only man in the column with exaggerated hopefulness.

When the Abyssinian frontier was reached at Fer-Fer, and the lorries drawn up in a defensive perimeter for the night, Juma's officer began to feel very strongly that a guinea-fowl would taste very much better than bully-beef for dinner. So in the cool of the evening he sauntered off with his shot-gun to see what could be done about it.

Sergeant Oparo, as it happened, also had an urge for food, only it was no guinea-fowl he craved, but Somali sheep. So he, too, wandered off in the cool of the evening. He went toward a Somali bivouac, accompanied by a few of his cronies armed with bayonets. They had all quite forgotten what their Bwana officer had so often told them about the need to win the friendship of the fierce Somali tribes.

Half an hour later there broke out a most shocking pandemonium as Sergeant Oparo, a sheep over his shoulder and his clothes bespattered with blood, came rushing into the perimeter with his panic-stricken Wakamba followers at his heels.

Following them, brandishing long spears, were about a hundred frantic Somali warriors with no desire in the world except to stick those spears through Wakamba entrails.

Bwana Sergeant Robinson, with Juma and his Baganda, ran forward to stand between hunters and hunted. The Somalis, not yet quite worked up to the pitch of killing a white man, came to a halt and contented themselves for the moment with wild yells and gesticulations.

This was the tableau that greeted the Bwana officer as he returned to the camp with two fat guinea-fowl for his evening meal. As soon as he saw it his air of content vanished and he strode forward.

"What's wrong?" he demanded.

"It seems that Oparo has had a little bother with the Somalis, sir," explained Sergeant Robinson.

The Somali din had died down on the officer's approach. He addressed them. "Do any of you speak Swahili?"

"No, sahib, but I speak English", replied one of the chiefs. "I one time belong British Somaliland Camel Corps."

"Then explain the meaning of all this fuss, but first tell your men not to threaten with their spears."

This done, the Somali chief told his story.

"Sahib, one of our herds he looking after sheep when some of your askaris find him. They not know we close in the bush, but pick up a sheep. Herd he say 'no, you mustn't steal sheep', so one askari take bayonet and stab herd through shoulder. Then run away with sheep. Sahib we all see this stabbing."

"Where is your wounded man?"

He was produced at once. The officer took out iodine, gauze and bandages and expertly bound the wound.

"How much was the sheep worth?" he asked, the operation over. A price was named, whereupon the officer produced the money from his pocket, to which he added a further and larger sum as a solace for the injured herd.

"We are your friends", he said. "I regret this business. Tell that to your men."

The chief did so and the Somalis looked pleased. They pressed forward to shake the officer's hand, but he had other business to transact.

"Can you identify the askari who did the stabbing?"

"Yes, sahib. He had three stripes on his arm – a sergeant, sahib."

"Very well. Thank you very much for your help. That is all."

The Somalis held up their arms in salute and took their leave, whereupon the officer went to his car and fetched a kiboko. He had hoped that he would never have had occasion to use it.

He sent for Sergeant Oparo and his mind was cold with rage.

As the sounds of the subsequent proceedings fell upon Juma's ears he snorted with contempt for the culprit.

"That is what should happen to all Wakamba maniacs who make affairs", he said.

"Truly", replied Matua. "Truly."

To neither of them did the thought occur: "There, but for the grace of God, howl I."

## XXIII. REGENERATION

The subaltern had no authority to take away Sergeant Oparo's stripes, let alone use the kiboko on him. Had there been a barrack-room lawyer in his section – fortunately this species is rare among Africans – there might well have followed a court-martial in the months to come, perhaps even dismissal from the service. He understood the risks he took.

No less did he understand why he took them. His job was to carry ammunition to the forward brigade through the wild and hazardous deserts of the Ogaden. No infantry accompanied his lorries as escort. One incident, such as the stealing of the sheep and the stabbing of the herd, was sufficient to inflame the fierce Ogaden Somalis and bring them hurtling down in thousands to destroy his convoy. What then would happen to his men, his vehicles, his precious loads of ammunition upon which the lives of the brigade reaching far forward into a hostile country might depend?

He had consigned the regulations where under such circumstances they belonged.

Next day he sent for Corporal Muli, a Jaluo with a clean copy-book except for about a dozen minor blots, and without any undue optimism made him acting sergeant in Oparo's place. That done, he summoned Juma.

"Juma", he said. "I am going to give you another chance as an N.C.O."

"Oh thank you Effendi, thank you very much." His smile of joy swallowed up the rest of his face.

"You will get back two stripes. If your behave yourself I expect you will get the third back in time. But there must be no more damn silly shauris. "

"No, Effendi, I will make no more affairs. This is a very long and difficult safari, Effendi, and I shall do my best to help you, for if it be left to the Wakamba wart-hogs we shall be dead men."

"The Wakamba are good men in their way, Corporal Juma, just as you all are. But like the rest of you they are liable to go stark raving mad. Tell Sergeant Muli that we move off in half an hour."

"Thank you, Effendi, thank you very much."

As Juma went to deliver the message his mind was too full of the sunbeams of happiness to give much attention to the Bwana officer's grave aberration in classing him among the Wakamba maniacs. In fact by this time he rejoined his brother he was convinced that this officer had said exactly the opposite.

"Listen, O Matua!" he exclaimed. "I am again to be a corporal. The Bwana officer has said that unless I have authority to deal with their madness the Wakamba jackals will make dead men of us all. He said that it is I alone who never make affairs."

Matua's honest fraternal heart rejoiced in Juma's reviving fortunes. "And the reward?" he asked. "Did the Bwana officer say anything about the reward for our great Battle of the River?"

"Truly", replied Juma. "The Bwana officer took me by the arm, as is the custom of white men among themselves, and he said, "You understand Juma, why you have not yet had your big reward? It is because all our lorries must carry ammunition and I cannot yet send them to England to fetch the gifts. But when we have finished with the Italiani in the country of the Habashi, and when we have more tyres and springs – for the gifts will be heavy – then I shall take all the garis on the long safari to England and you will become one of the richest men in the world."

Matua made a purring noise. In his mind's eye he could already see that superb convoy on the march.

But Juma's romanticism did not get in the way of his doing an excellent job of work in the arduous days to come.

A few minutes later the convoy was moving across the frontier of the Ogaden and climbing the escarpments which rose suddenly out of the coastal plain.

The Italians, intending to build a road across these desolate wastes had blasted a passage round the sides of the hills, but not having time to finish the work, they had left giant boulders bestrewing the way. Similarly they had transported millions of tons of flints for the intervening highway across the deserts, but these had become bedded beneath the deposits of daily sandstorms, so that only by the greatest courtesy could the route taken by the convoy be called a track.

The drivers would find themselves climbing precipitous ledges and skirting preposterous boulders that often left but an inch between them and a swerve to violent death hundreds of feet below. Across the desert plateau beyond, the sand would subside beneath their wheels, so that axles and petrol-tanks fell with a sickening bump against the rocks and flints.

Punctures were frequent, tyres were ripped open, petrol tanks and sumps pierced or dented, steering damaged, brakes impaired, springs broken and tied together with wire – and when this gave out, with string.

Every evening, when the head of the convoy had halted for sleep, the Bwana sergeant would be working desperately hard upon broken down lorries far in the rear. Every evening he would look up and see a lorry ploughing towards him from the front. It was Juma, voluntarily coming back to help.

Sometimes on the march the Bwana officer, seeking easier passage for his vehicles would lead them along the dry-bed of a water course, and when the surface here collapsed, or became too thickly strewn with boulders, he would lead them back again to the agony of the hidden flints.

At other times, when the ground was sufficiently unbroken, he would order the lorries to advance in line abreast, so that each driver might escape the blinding dust of the vehicle in front. On one such occasion a sand-storm arose and lasted for an hour. When it died down, restoring vision, the convoy commander could have wept. Some of his lorries could be seen disappearing over the horizon on the left flank; others were haring off miles away to the right flank; others again were even to be seen observed retreating obliquely miles to the rear. As though the choking dust and the pulverising heat and the impossible country were not sufficient ordeal, he now had to drive off to rope them all in, with a party on board his car to lift it out each time it sank into the sand.

After three exhausting hours he came back with all the strayed sheep from the right flank, and was preparing to set off after those on the left flank when he was amazed to see them coming in, apparently under their own volition.

But appearances were deceptive. It proved to be the work of the excellent Juma. The officer's heart warmed towards him and he wondered how there could ever have been the very slightest cause for complaint against him.

Soon afterwards, Bwana Sergeant Robinson arrived, begrimed like all the rest. Looking out at the vast expanse of yellow nothingness – they were hundreds of miles from anywhere – the sergeant said to his officer in his honest north-country dialect.

"They don't seem to get Corporation water-cart round here, sir. I reckon they be silly baskets in these parts to pay their rates."

The officer laughed – a surprising sound these days.

"Why does the Bwana officer laugh?" asked Matua wonderingly.

"He laughs", said Juma, "because of his joy that I help him like a brother."

# XXIV. ACCLAMATION

Like a tiny ship battling though a vast expanse of ocean the ammunition convoy creaked and groaned and laboured through the Ogaden wilds until gradually the barren yellows and grey tints of the bush began to give way to green and until at last, in the cool of a glorious evening, the lorries recaptured their old content as they sped purring over the grasslands of the great Jiggiga plains and reached the brigade without accident or loss.

The Brigadier was pleased. "Well done", he said to the convoy commander. "We did not expect you for another thirty-six hours at least. Now we shall be able to have a crack at those blighters up there." He pointed to the mountain barrier which stood guard over Abyssinia proper, where the lights of innumerable camp fires indicated that the Italian host was gathered, ready to defend the heights.

Next day the drivers had a grand-stand view of the fighting as the Nigerian infantry deployed over the plain and advanced to the attack in what was to become known as the Battle of Marda Pass. It was a bitter fight, but in the end the British forced the position and the Nigerians went on to storm the Babilli Gap some several miles further into the mountains.

And then the God of Battles gathered together all the strings of destiny, rolled them into a ball, and placed the ball in the hands of none other than the hero of this narrative. The hour had arrived when Juma was to win undying fame.

His officer had been forward with the infantry at Babilli and returned towards evening with orders to bring his convoy forward, but first to despatch one lorry at utmost speed loaded with small arms ammunition. The idea of the infantry was to press on before the

Italians could consolidate their third position in the formidable mountains that stood athwart the gates of Harrar.

Juma was entrusted with the task of driving this special lorry. He was given full instructions, particularly with regard to the track-junction at Babilli. Here he must veer off to the right and on no account keep to the main road. Did he understand?

Yes Effendi, thank you very much indeed, he understood perfectly.

"And go at top speed", enjoined the officer.

"Oh thank you very much indeed, Effendi." Never before had Juma received such an order, never before had he known such an order given. The injunction before had always been to drive slowly and carefully. He felt as a man might feel who had been given a blank cheque by a millionaire. He was overjoyed at so superb an opportunity to become himself a millionaire of speed.

In a few moments he was off. The last stretch of the Jiggiga plains fled past him and he roared up the slopes towards Marda, passed the battlefield at fifty miles an hour, and with a crazy skill dodged great rocks blasted down upon the road. The switchback beyond he took at sixty and hurtled past Babilli at a good seventy. So intoxicating was this ecstasy that other instructions faded from his mind. He forgot the little matter about turning to the right and kept on the main road at a royal speed, never in his life having experienced such flawless happiness.

Half a dozen miles past Babilli he swung round a bend and that instant his happiness vanished, to make room for an equally perfect terror. For he beheld in front of him on the narrow mountain road, here made narrower still by demolitions, a huge column on the march. They were Italians on the way back to man their new defences. Juma's eyes bulged. To turn was out of the question as to reverse, for one side was a sheer vertical wall of rock and on the other an appalling precipice. Panic seized him. He did not know what he was doing, but what he did do was to press his foot down still further on the accelerator and hurtle forward into the Italian hosts.

There were shouts and shrieks and squeals of alarm as the enemy tried to scatter. Many were mown down by the lorries incredible amok run. Others in desperation flung themselves to certain death over the precipice. But most managed to flatten themselves against the vertical wall and thus saved themselves from annihilation by less than half a mudguard's breadth.

Juma swept on like an avenging fury past the flattened column, kept his vehicle on the ledge by virtue of the most fantastic luck, and eventually emerged from the defile into a space wide enough to permit of a circuit, if one wished to turn about. And Juma, his eyes bulging more than ever, wished for nothing in the wide world except to make the turn. Even though it meant running the Italian gauntlet a second time, he had no other thought than to speed back safely into the arms of his own kith and kin and the beautiful security of the British lines. He had heard rumours of what Italian troops did to their prisoners and he did not like what he had heard.

So he took the circuit without slackening speed and came roaring back along the road.

This was altogether too much for the shaken Italians. They had survived one death-dealing charge by this maniac lorry, and that it should now be returning to attack them from the front revealed an insane grandeur of courage that seemed not to belong to this world. They could not be expected to fight against an elemental god embattled in a modern chariot. They threw away their rifles to a man and held up their hands.

As Juma approached and saw a long forest of arms accosting him in surrender his presence of mind returned with remarkable promptitude and his heart blazed with joy. Was this not yet another of his staggering victories? Indeed, was it not the greatest victory ever won by man? He brought his lorry to violent halt at the head of the

*" Juma swept like an avenging fury "*

column, seized his rifle, dismounted and ordered the Italian commander into the seat besides him. He next indicated to the white officers and N.C.O.s that they should get into the back of the vehicle. This done, he stood on the running board to gain height and made a sign to a sign to the colonial troops to turn about, and when they obeyed he resumed his place and drove on, herding the vast concourse of colonial troops in front of him at a steady run. As his enthusiasm increased so did his speed and soon his steady trot became a gallop along the narrow ledge of the pass.

By this time the rest of the convoy had joined the infantry at Babilli and a traffic-control at the junction where Juma had gone astray, although amazed at the sight, kept his head and directed the fantastic cavalcade in the right direction.

The Brigadier and two Colonels and – among others – Juma's Bwana officer were talking together in the British lines, when they saw to their astonishment an enemy column, hundreds in number, come charging among them with their hands held aloft, and far in the rear one British lorry crammed with Italian officers – a solitary sheep-dog.

A roar of cheering broke out from every part of the camp.

Juma acknowledged it with a matter-of-fact air of one to whom such triumphs are as common as one's daily bully-beef and biscuits.

# XXV. TEMPTATION

When the advance was continued along the mountain road, officers of the Italian army came out to meet the British column and to surrender to them the walled city of Harrar, second largest town in their Abyssinian Empire.

Juma was in no doubt about the meaning behind the sudden collapse of enemy opposition; it was because the thunder of his name and legend again throbbed in Italian ears and robbed their hearts of courage. Who could withstand the onslaught of a mighty hero who had gained such epic victories in the Battle of the River and in the mountain fastness of the country of the Habashi!

As he drove in the vanguard his mind recalled the triumphant evening when he had driven the enemy hosts before him into the British camp. There had been an immediate summons to the presence of the Bwana Mkubwa Sana – the red-tabbed Brigadier – with whom many other officers, including his own, were standing. His own Bwana officer questioned him.

"What is this thing that has happened, Corporal Juma?" he asked.

"Effendi", he replied. "It is a very good thing. I was driving with the ammunition as you told me, and I was ready to take the turning to the right which you had ordered when I saw a great army of the Italiani coming along the road to kill the army of the Inglesi, so I drove straight into them, Effendi, and we had a big battle and when they saw they could not win they put up their hands and said in a voice of much fear – 'We can do battle no longer, for it is the great Juma himself who fights.'"

Juma's Bwana officer by this time had acquired a settled habit of scepticism and was about to go further into the matter when the

Brigadier eagerly demanded to know what Juma had said. The M.T. officer interpreted, without butting in with his own doubts.

"By Gad, remarkable!" exclaimed the Brigadier. "An amazingly plucky fellow, this corporal of yours."

The captured Italian commander, standing near at hand agreed. "Yes, my General", he said. "He is a soldier of the utmost valour."

"There, that's a first-hand corroboration", went on the Brigadier, delighted. "Look here my lad, I'll tell you what we'll do. You send in his name and number and I'll get him put up for a decoration, hanged if I won't. Tell him that!"

The M.T. officer obeyed. Juma's face became as radiant as the tropical sun. "Oh thank you Effendi. Thank you very, very much indeed". He saluted with both hands, bowed, retreated, turned to bow and salute again, and then ran as far as his legs could carry him to tell Matua.

His Bwana officer, sauntering off to his evening meal, turned the remarkable episode over in his mind. "All the same", he said to himself. "I don't think it happened quite like that – no, not by a long way. Yet hang it all, the prisoners are real enough, and so was the tribute of that Italian colonel. I don't know – I give it up".

Under the circumstances he thought it would be pedantic and ungracious to read Juma a lecture on not keeping on the right route, and so on this score he forever held his peace.

When the British saw the walled city of Harrar at their feet their hearts leapt high, while the heart of Juma leapt right over the moon. They camped on the high ground above the town and in the afternoon Sergeant Muli, the Jaluo, slid off unobserved. He returned an hour later and sought out the grand Juma, whom he wished to propitiate. "Listen Juma", he said. "I bring great tidings, for I have bought some bhang."

Juma sat up, instantly alert. "Bhang", he exclaimed. "That is very good."

"To-night" continued the sergeant "We shall enjoy much bhang, and then we shall go into this great city you have captured, that the women of the Habashi may see their conqueror."

Juma agreed with enthusiasm: it seemed only fair to the women. So Sergeant Muli presented him with a fistful of brown weeds and withdrew, with a rendezvous fixed for that night.

Towards evening Juma's Bwana officer happened to send for him. "Oh Juma", he said. "Let me have your pay-book. I've got to re-enter your corporal's pay."

Juma pulled out his pay-book and as he did so, the brown weeds simultaneously emerged from his pocket. His officer seized them.

"Really, Juma", he said. "You are the biggest fool I've ever met. Here you have everything in your grasp and you want to throw the whole damned thing away by turning yourself into a maniac. I'm going to burn this stuff, and to-night you'll report to me every hour until I go to bed. Then you will report every hour to the infantry guard. Enough."

Juma went off, disconsolate and angry, but not daring to disobey. He remembered the affair of Sergeant Oparo.

Sergeant Muli, suffering under no prohibition, smoked bhang on his own. Then he took his lorry off in the dead of night, drove into the forbidden city, scattering the guards, raced along the narrow streets until he entered one too narrow to accommodate his passage, knocked down two mud houses and finally wedged the vehicle between two more houses with such firmness that it refused to move forwards or backwards.

Having thus by accident rendered it immobile, he went off on foot to woo the ladies of the Habashi, and his comrades never saw him alive again. When they did find him – but, the incident is not a pretty enough one to be described here.

Corporal Juma was in the search-party that discovered first the vehicle, and then its driver. The latter sight made him reflect very deeply.

Next day the column dropped down the almost vertical incline into Diredawa and on halting Juma went to his Bwana officer.

"Effendi", he said. "About the affair of last night – I want to thank you, Effendi."

"O.K.", replied the officer. "But remember that I can't always be your ruddy nurse. Meanwhile you can have your third stripe back."

"Of course", said Juma later to Matua. "A man who was fool enough to do what Muli did deserved what he got. I warned him of the danger, but like a madman he would take no notice. Only a man with a strong head like me should smoke bhang.

"Truly", agreed Matua, "You have a wonderfully strong head."

## XXVI. CONSUMATION

Unfortunately for Juma's Bwana officer, on the last three hundred miles to the Abyssinian capital he was carrying the infantry whom he had transported across the Somaliland frontier – the infantry commanded by the Colonel with the twirling moustachios, whose delight was now to watch out for something to go wrong, and whose deep disgruntlement it was that nothing did go wrong.

The terrain across which they laboured, though nothing compared to the Ogaden or the wastes of Jubaland, was yet full of difficulty. It gave the appearance of having been ploughed up by a giant, the lorries climbing and descending deep ravines that stretched ahead in endless succession. By this time some of the vehicles could travel only in first gear, others in top. Clutches were worn out, so were brake-drums. There were no spare parts. Water in the radiators was constantly boiling over.

Yet these vertical dongas were taken without accident. No vehicle had to be abandoned. No infantry passenger sustained damage. It was a triumph of driving which the Colonel would not admit, but could not gainsay.

Finally the advance entered upon the highland plains and went whizzing over the firm black soil to the very gates of Addis Ababa. Preparations were at once made for the triumphant entry.

Juma's Bwana officer was summoned to the presence of Colonel Moustachio who forthwith addressed him.

"My battalion will march in to-morrow on foot. You will stay here with your lorries until I send for you, and mind you keep your bloody scoundrels in order this time, do you understand."

"I understand your instructions, sir, but I take exception to your language."

"What the devil do you mean?"

"I mean that my men have given you good service and ought not to be blackguarded, sir."

"You're under arrest", bellowed the Colonel.

"I beg to point out that I have been under arrest by you for some time, sir. To-morrow, I shall seek an interview with the G.O.C."

"Clear out", roared the Colonel. The M.T. officer saluted and went.

The drivers were disconsolate that they should be kept out of the triumphant march into Addis. Juma, watching the infantry set forth on foot, took it as a personal insult.

Parked near to them was a Cape coloured M.T. Company, similarly abandoned. In the afternoon a Cape coloured corporal and some cronies came over and talked in Swahili with Juma.

"Have you any empty petrol debbies, Sergeant?" asked the man from the Cape.

"Plenty" replied Juma.

"Good". Send out some men to sell them to the Habashi for milk. Then we shall have a good drink."

Juma laughed scornfully. "Milk!"

"Do not laugh. Buy some milk and we'll use our sugar ration. We'll mix up the milk and sugar with Italian petrol. Man, it makes a lovely drink."

An hour later the Baganda and the Cape men were as near delirium as makes no odds.

"Why should we be left behind, we who have done all the work?" demanded the Cape corporal, his eyes rolling.

"Why should I be kept out of the city I have captured with my own hands?" demanded Juma, with eyes even more fantastically a-wash.

"We shall walk in by ourselves", said the Cape corporal.

"We shall drive in my lorry", corrected Juma.

Baganda and Cape men surged upon the lorry and a few minutes later, Juma at the wheel, they were roaring under the railway arch and along the great switchback which is the main street of Addis Ababa.

Towards the far end life took on something of the tempo of a busy city. Vast crowds were swarming along the pavements and Juma's blurred vision caught glimpses of innumerable white civilians.

"Who are these white people?" he demanded.

"Why man", replied the Cape corporal. "They are Italians."

"Italians!" Juma was amazed. "Italians! Enemies of the King of the Inglesi. At large! With nobody doing anything to kill them." His warrior soul was shocked. He must make good the deficiency. A glimpse of Bwana Sergeant Robinson among the crowd confirmed him in his decision. The Bwana sergeant who made the affair of the water was his enemy and therefore the enemy of the King of the Inglesi. He would repeat his tactics of the mountain battle. He would charge with his lorry and liquidate the whole boiling shooting match. He would crown his fame in the very streets of Addis.

"Stop man!" roared the corporal.

"Stop" yelled the passengers on the back.

But Juma was stopping for nobody. Amid yells of terror from the crowd, and a panic-stricken flight before his mad career, he drove at full tilt for the crowds on the pavement, smashed into a shop, and overturned his lorry.

It was a most spectacular crash. The crowds gathered round in their thousands, as is the way of crowds. Juma crawling out from the cab – he was much too drunk to have hurt himself – saw them assembled in front of him. Clearly they had collected to acclaim their conqueror. He climbed upon the wreck of his lorry.

"Listen all you people", he called out. "Do you know who I am? I am Juma. I am the great Juma himself."

Two grim British military policeman pushed a way through and Juma swayed ecstatically into their arms. As he was being led away he turned back to explain to the crowd what was happening.

"These policemen have been sent by the King of the Inglesi to fetch me for my reward", he shouted happily. "The King of the Inglesi is my brother."

# XXVII. DECORATION


Juma's Bwana sergeant, who had witnessed the whole sorry episode, secured a working party to turn the lorry the right way up, improvised a few rapid repairs, collected the bruised, shaken and now largely sober members of the truant party, and drove them back to his company's lines outside Addis.

"Where's Juma?" asked his officer, when they arrived.

The sergeant explained.

"This *would* happen" exclaimed the officer. "What do you think I have here? A chit saying that Juma has been awarded the African Star for Gallantry! And now he goes and messes the whole thing up. Typical of his conduct throughout the campaign."

The Company Commander strolled along and the situation was outlined for his benefit.

"Well, what do we about it?" he asked, with twinkling eyes. "Do we help a very gallant black gentleman in his hour of need, or do we leave the scoundrel to his deserts?"

"I don't know so much about the gallant black gentleman", said Juma's officer. "His exploits have always seemed to me quite remarkably phoney, although I can't explain why. Still Providence is clearly on his side, and who are we to go against Providence?"

"Is there to be an investiture?" asked the Company Commander.

"Yes, the day after to-morrow."

"Then you haven't much time to lose if you intend to conspire to defeat the ends of justice by producing his heroic body. Not, of course, that I could countenance such a thing." And the Major walked off with a chuckle.

The sergeant regarded his retreating back.

"Would you say that was a hint, sir?" he asked the officer.

"I would" replied the officer grinning. "Any ideas?"

"You don't happen to have a spare bottle of whisky sir, do you?"

"Whatever for?"

"The military police have had a tiring day. They might like to celebrate the capture of Addis, if you take my meaning sir."

"Look here, my lad, I won't be a party to corrupting the military police", said the officer.

"You can't corrupt them blighters, sir", replied the sergeant with conviction. The officer allowed the equivocal remark to pass without comment.

When evening came the sergeant set forth by car to encompass the rescue of Juma. Concealed on the seat beside him was a bottle of whisky.

The military police at the Bulari post, where Juma had been taken, exhausted by the labours of the day, were in a sultry mood. They asked the M.T. sergeant what he wanted.

"I've come for the body of one Juma", he told them.

"That crazy Wog!" exclaimed the Provost-sergeant, "I've just made out five charges against him."

"My officers want me to take custody of him", said Juma's sergeant. "He'll have to come up before them first anyway."

"You don't get him until the A.P.M. issues orders", announced the provost sergeant firmly. "And that may be in a week's time."

"It's all one to me", said Sergeant Robinson. "I don't want the perisher on my hands all evening. I'm going to celebrate."

"That's a good one!" said the provost sergeant with a bitter laugh. "Celebrate in this place! What with?"

"A drop of Scotch."

"Scotch in Addis! Hear that, Corporal Smith? He's going to find Scotch in this lousy hole! Ha, ha, ha!"

"I've brought my own supplies", said the sly Sergeant Robinson.

That put an entirely different light on the situation. Two hours later, the body of Juma, previously to be hoarded like precious treasure, was handed over, still in rather an inebriated condition, to his rescuer with a gesture of open-hearted generosity.

"Take him and cherish him", said the Provost Sergeant in a slightly thickening voice. "Cherish him like the sweetheart he is. I'll send charge-sheet to A.P.M 'morrow morning o' boy."

"Couldn't I take the charge-sheet, too, o' boy?" asked Sergeant Robinson. "My officer wants to see exactly what this perisher has been up to. You can have it back in the morning."

"Wan' charge-sheet, too? Shertainly o'boy. Take it with my love and blessing." The Provost-Sergeant in that elated hour would have made a present of the sun, moon and stars.

On the way back Juma awoke from his stupor and began chanting a war song.

"Shut up!" shouted the sergeant.

Juma took this as encouragement to continue. The sergeant, with business-like precision, stopped the engine, turned to Juma, cracked him on the jaw, started the engine and drove on in peace, his protégé having once more lapsed into stupor.

For the next thirty-six hours Juma was watched with a devoted care such as he had never encountered, even at his mother's knee. He could no step in any direction without four picked men keeping him company.

Meanwhile a fatigue party had been organised to wash him and his clothes, to polish his belt and boots, and generally to ensure that he should appear on parade as a paragon among soldiers. Juma was very astonished. He had no idea why such a fuss was being made, and care was taken not to put the key to the mystery in his hands.

On the morning of the appointed day the company was fallen in and marched to the parade-ground, where it was joined by detachments from other units. The parade was drawn up to form three sides of a square. A Very High Officer – of a Highness Juma had never before encountered – arrived on the scene. Arms were presented. The salute was returned. Arms were sloped and then ordered.

Juma, to his utter amazement, was ordered to march forward twenty paces. As he complied, panic clutched at his heart. "It is the affair of the overturned lorry", he muttered to himself. "These white men can never leave anything alone. They must always make affairs. The Bwana Mkubwa Sana has come to punish me with a terrible punishment."

He stood waiting. An interpreter was placed by his side.

The Very High Officer asked that the parade should stand at ease. Then, clearing his throat, he began to speak.

"While we expect a high level of courage from every soldier", he said, "there will always be some men who reveal themselves as outstandingly plucky. Such a man now stands before us. Sergeant Juma, in the name of the General Officer Commanding I award you the African Star for Gallantry."

He pinned the glittering decoration on Juma's breast.

It was some time before Juma took in what was happening. The Bwana Mkubwa Sana shook hands with him. Juma was staggered.

Then realisation came to him. He beamed with a radiance which increased the torrid heat of the day. He looked at his breast and saw the medal there. And then he looked up again and saw the sun; the sun was but a reflection of his medal.

He was too moved to say a word, even had one been required of him. "Salute!" said his own Bwana officer in a hoarse, urgent whisper.

Juma did not hear. He looked down at his breast again and his breast seemed to swell and swell until it covered all Africa and then all the King's domains.

The King's Domains? Why, thought Juma, the Bwana Mkubwa Sana must be none other than the King of the Inglesi in person! And then, with a series of sumptuous salutes, he assured Bwana Mkubwa Sana that he would fight all his enemies and destroy them utterly, for was he not Juma the Great? Let all British forces be disbanded. As, single-handed, he had overthrown the Italiani so would he destroy the wicked Germani. There was no need for other men.

"What does he say?" asked the Very High Officer.

"He thanks you, sir, and says he will always do his best", said Juma's Bwana, hastening to intervene before the interpreter could speak.

"Stout fellow!" exclaimed the Very High Officer.

Juma was marched back to the ranks. He went preceded by his glittering chest and with as much martial glory inside him as the heart of man can bear.

And, perhaps, with rather more.

"I am Juma the Great", he confided to Matua when he rejoined the ranks.

"Kweli", replied the adoring Matua. "Truly you are Juma the Great."

**THE END**

# "Black Beauty" - A Review of *Juma the Great* from *Truth*, September 1947.

Those who have hitherto only known Mr. A.K. Chesterton as the writer of fiery polemics, the chastiser with scorpions of fools and Socialists—he would probably say the terms are synonymous—will find in this good-humoured and humorous book quite another Mr. Chesterton.

Juma, in Uganda, is cajoled into becoming a recruit in a mechanised column in 1940. He is enticed chiefly by the glorious prospect of wearing "a big askari hat," but also largely by the anticipatory delight of driving a lorry and achieving great honour and glory, plus one hundred "shillingi" a month with which, later, to buy more wives.

From that starting point the story is ostensibly of Juma's adventures and misadventures—and to an addict of bhang misadventures are inevitable—but it is really a study in the queer lovable psychology and the mental misconceptions of this child of nature.

The tale is told with much of the early Kipling savour and understanding; it carries a faint reminiscence of the magic of Wallace's *Bosambo* stories, but it is entirely individual.

Mr. Chesterton leavens his riotous fun with a certain cynicism, and occasionally drops out a dictum or draws a pen portrait which redeems the tale from the category of mere farcical narration. His knowledge of the native psyche is uncanny; his understanding of the British officers no less penetrating. "The proper study of mankind is man" might fitly have been the title-page motto, for underlying all the hilarity is a tenderness saved from awkwardness, or the bitterness which tenderness so often generates, by the consistency of the author's technique.

# About A.K. Chesterton

Arthur Kenneth Chesterton was born at the Luipaards Vlei gold mine, Krugersdorp, South Africa where his father was an official in 1899.

In 1915 unhappy at school in England A.K. returned to South Africa. There and without the knowledge of his parents, and having exaggerated his age by four years, he enlisted in the 5th South African Infantry.

Before his 17th birthday he had been in the thick of three battles in German East Africa. Later in the war he transferred as a commissioned officer to the Royal Fusiliers and served for the rest of the war on the Western Front being awarded the Military Cross in 1918 for conspicuous gallantry.

Between the wars A.K. first prospected for diamonds before becoming a journalist first in South Africa and then England. Alarmed at the economic chaos threatening Britain, he joined Sir Oswald Mosley in the B.U.F and became prominent in the movement. In 1938, he quarrelled with Mosley's policies and left the movement.

When the Second World War started he rejoined the army, volunteered for tropical service and went through all the hardships of the great push up from Kenya across the wilds of Jubaland through the desert of the Ogaden and into the remotest parts of Somalia. He was afterwards sent down the coast to join the Somaliland Camel Corps and intervene in the inter-tribal warfare among the Somalis.

In 1943 his health broke down and he was invalided out of the army with malaria and colitis, returning to journalism. In 1944, he became deputy editor and chief leader writer of *Truth*.

In the early 1950s A.K. established *Candour* and founded the League of Empire Loyalists which for some years made many colourful headlines in the press worldwide. He later took that organisation into The National Front, and served as its Chairman for a time.

A.K. Chesterton died in 1973.

**A.K. Chesterton**

# About The A.K. Chesterton Trust

*The A.K. Chesterton Trust* was formed by Colin Todd and the late Miss. Rosine de Bounevialle in January 1996 to succeed and continue the work of the now defunct Candour Publishing Co.

The objects of the Trust are stated as follows:

**"To promote and expound the principles of A.K. Chesterton which are defined as being to demonstrate the power of, and to combat the power of International Finance, and to promote the National Sovereignty of the British World."**

Our aims include:

- *Maintaining and expanding the range of material relevant to A.K. Chesterton and his associates throughout his life.*

- *To preserve and keep in-print important works on British Nationalism in order to educate the current generation of our people.*

- *The maintenance and recovery of the sovereign independence of the British Peoples throughout the world.*

- *The strengthening of the spiritual and material bonds between the British Peoples throughout the world.*

- *The resurgence at home and abroad of the British spirit.*

We will raise funds by way of merchandising and donations.

We ask that our friends make provision for *The A.K. Chesterton Trust* in their will.

The A.K. Chesterton Trust has a **duty** to keep *Candour* in the ring and punching.


**CANDOUR: To defend national sovereignty against the menace of international finance.**

**CANDOUR: To serve as a link between Britons all over the world in protest against the surrender of their world heritage.**

# Subscribe to Candour

**CANDOUR SUBSCRIPTION RATES FOR 10 ISSUES.**

U.K. £30.00
Europe 50 Euros.
Rest of the World £45.00.
USA $60.00.

All Airmail. Cheques and Postal Orders, £'s Sterling only, made payable to *The A.K. Chesterton Trust*. (Others, please send cash by **secure post**, $ bills or Euro notes.)

Payment by Paypal is available. Please see our website **www.candour.org.uk** for more information.

# Candour Back Issues

**Back issues are available. 1953 to the present.**

Please request our back issue catalogue by sending your name and address with two 1st class stamps to:

**The A.K. Chesterton Trust, BM Candour, London, WC1N 3XX, UK**

Alternatively, see our website at **www.candour.org.uk** where you can order a growing selection on-line.

# *The A.K. Chesterton Trust* Reprint Series

1. Creed of a Fascist Revolutionary & Why I Left Mosley - A.K. Chesterton.

2. The Menace of World Government & Britain's Graveyard - A.K. Chesterton.

3. What You Should Know About The United Nations - The League of Empire Loyalists.

4. The Menace of the Money-Power - A.K. Chesterton.

5. The Case for Economic Nationalism - John Tyndall.

6. Sound the Alarm! - A.K. Chesterton.

7. Six Principles of British Nationalism - John Tyndall.

8. B.B.C. - A National Menace - A.K. Chesterton.

9. Stand by the Empire - A.K. Chesterton.

10. Tomorrow. A Plan for the British Future - A.K. Chesterton.

11. The British Constitution and the Corruption of Parliament - Ben Greene.

# Other Titles from *The A.K. Chesterton Trust*

Leopard Valley - A.K. Chesterton.

Juma The Great - A.K. Chesterton.

The New Unhappy Lords - A.K. Chesterton.

Facing The Abyss - A.K. Chesterton.

The History of the League of Empire Loyalists - McNeile & Black

**All the above titles are available from The A.K. Chesterton Trust, BM Candour, London, WC1N 3XX, UK**

**www.candour.org.uk**

www.ingramcontent.com/pod-product-compliance
Lightning Source LLC
Chambersburg PA
CBHW060428260626
47161CB00005B/1829